Simon's stare made Maggie feel self-conscious.

"What is it? Do I have dirt on me nose?" she said finally. Her stomach was in knots, and she couldn't erase the way she'd felt last night in Simon's arms.

His eyes widened, and he grinned. "Sorry. Was I staring? You look lovely today, Maggie. I'm getting used to your short hair."

Heat flooded Maggie's face. "But sure, and I think you've kissed the Blarney stone!" She rubbed her short hair. " 'Tis hideous, I know. But it will grow." Warmth flooded her at his words.

"You could never be hideous, Maggie." Simon came closer and touched her hair with a light touch. "It's as soft as it looks. And so curly."

Maggie felt as though her tongue had stuck fast to the roof of her mouth.

"I talked to my lawyer friend today," he said.

Maggie caught her breath. "What did he say?"

"We could try to persuade the court to make Fiona a ward of someone who would allow her to stay with you and supervise her care. Or you could be married."

"M–married?"

Simon's eyes were somber, and he nodded.

Maggie felt as though she couldn't breathe. In that moment she knew she wanted nothing more from her life than to marry the man standing before her. She loved the way he studied a situation before making a decision, the way he had of standing with his hands in his pockets, the little cowlick on the left side of his head. Most of all she loved his steadfastness. Once he loved a woman, he would be committed to her and to her only, for the rest of his life. A woman would never have to wonder where she stood with Sheriff Simon Masters.

That woman would be the luckiest woman in the world. And it wouldn't be Maggie O'Keefe. Unshed tears burned Maggie's throat, and she quickly turned away.

COLLEEN COBLE and her husband, David, raised two great kids, David Jr., and Kara, and they are now knee-deep in paint and wallpaper chips as they restore a Victorian home. Colleen became a Christian after a bad car accident in 1980, when all her grandmother's prayers finally took root. She is very active at her church, where she sings and helps her husband with a Sunday school class. She writes inspirational romance because she believes that the only happily ever after is with God at the center. She now works as a church secretary but would like to eventually pursue her writing full-time.

Books by Colleen Coble

HEARTSONG PRESENTS
HP271—Where Leads the Heart
HP327—Plains of Promise
HP360—The Heart Answers
HP395—To Love a Stranger
HP417—From Russia with Love
HP429—Love Ahoy
HP456—The Cattle Baron's Wife

Don't miss out on any of our super romances. Write to us at the following address for information on our newest releases and club membership.

Heartsong Presents Readers' Service
PO Box 721
Uhrichsville, OH 44683

Or visit www.heartsongpresents.com

Maggie's Mistake

Colleen Coble

Heartsong Presents

For the Lifebuilders Sunday school class at New Life Baptist Church. You bring us much joy!

A note from the author:
I love to hear from my readers! You may correspond with me by writing:

> **Colleen Coble**
> **Author Relations**
> **PO Box 719**
> **Uhrichsville, OH 44683**

ISBN 1-58660-596-8

MAGGIE'S MISTAKE

All Scripture quotations are taken from the King James Version of the Bible.

All of the characters and events in this book are fictitious. Any resemblance to actual persons, living or dead, or to actual events is purely coincidental.

Cover design by Jeff McClintock.

PRINTED IN THE U.S.A.

one

Wagons rattled along the pothole-laden streets, their rumbling sounding like distant thunder. Maggie O'Keefe squinted as she peered out her clean windows, then went back to rolling the pie dough. This was the last of her orders for the day. A sense of pride squared her aching shoulders. They said it couldn't be done, those naysayers who pointed out all the other bakeries in town. They said she was a lone woman without a friend in this bustling town of Wabash, Indiana. To be successful in business, she would need friends and acquaintances. But she had proved them wrong. Word had soon spread through town that *Maggie's,* though down an alleyway off Miami Street, carried the best baked goods in town. And when the Irish community in nearby Lagro heard that one of their own served Irish pastries, even more customers poured in.

Maggie blew a red curl out of her eyes. "Fiona, bring me the cinnamon," she called. Her three-year-old sister had asked to play in the sandbox behind the shop, but Maggie knew her call would carry through the screen door behind her. She wiped the back of her hand across her cheek, then pushed a pie out of the way on the floured board before her. Drawing the bowl of apples toward her, she poured in some sugar and stirred. "Fiona, I'll be needing the cinnamon," she called again.

When there was no answer, she spun angrily on her heel and wiped her hands on her apron. Shouldering her way past the screen door, she stepped outside on the back stoop. Her gaze went to the sandbox. Empty. Frowning, she walked to the side of the building and looked down the side yard. She walked around the building calling her sister's name. There was no sign of Fiona. Maggie's heart began to pound, but she didn't panic. Not yet. Maybe Fiona had slipped up the back steps while Maggie was busy. Their apartment over the bakery, though small, was comfortable, and Fiona was probably tired after a full day of playing.

Gathering her skirts in her hand, Maggie hurried inside and up the stairs. "Fiona?" She pushed open the door to Fiona's room, but the cot was still made up neatly with the worn quilt Maggie had stitched when Fiona was born. She threw open the window facing the street and thrust her head out. Scanning the road and the yards beside it, she saw no sign of her sister.

Dread clutched at her throat, but she couldn't let it slow her down. Terrifying thoughts vied for control. The railway had brought strangers to town. She'd seen a strange man loitering at the Boston General Store yesterday. Someone could have seen Fiona alone and taken her. Or what if she'd wandered down by the canal and fallen in? The list went on and on in Maggie's head. Rushing down the front stairs, she exited in front of the display cabinet.

A man stood in the shop, his wide shoulders blocking her path through the doorway. Maggie was too upset to notice much about him other than the silver star on his jacket. The sheriff! Relief coursed through her.

"Oh, Sheriff, but sure, and you've got to help me! Fiona, she's only three," she babbled. " 'Tis sure I thought she'd stay in the backyard, but she's gone."

The sheriff's eyes narrowed, and in a moment he was out the door ahead of her. "We'll find her. What's she wearing?"

Maggie followed him onto the front stoop. "A blue dress and bonnet, but 'tis likely she's taken the bonnet off by now," she said in a rush. "She has red hair like mine."

The sheriff nodded and walked toward the canal calling Fiona's name. Terror gripped Maggie. Fiona knew better than to go to the canal. She forced herself to go in the opposite direction, stopping everyone who passed by on foot or by wagon or carriage, but no one had seen a little girl.

An hour later she trudged back to the house, her heart full of hope. Surely the sheriff had found her by now. But he was alone as he came toward her. Her heart sank, and she burst into tears.

"But sure, and we've got to find her—she's all I have left in the world," she said between tears. Maggie clutched the sheriff's coat and shook it. "You must find her!"

His warm brown eyes were sympathetic, but they held a bit of censure. "How did she wander off, Mrs.—? I'm sorry. I don't know your name."

"It's Maggie. Maggie O'Keefe." She barely noticed his address of her as missus. It wasn't important. Only Fiona mattered. "She was playing in the backyard. She's never wandered off before."

"Mrs. O'Keefe." He tipped his hat. "I'm Sheriff Simon

Masters. You said she was only three. That's too young to be allowed out without supervision. Young Timmy McDougal was run over by a wagon two weeks ago. His mother is grieving now, but it's too late. Children aren't toys to be played with and put down when you feel like it. They take a lot of care."

Outrage dried her tears, and Maggie drew herself to her full five feet five inches. " 'Tis sure you have no children, do you, Sheriff Masters?" He shook his head. "I thought not." Her Irish accent was thick with indignation. "Then don't be telling me I'm neglecting Fiona!" She held out her calloused hands. "I love Fiona, and I will work my fingers off to nubs to provide for her—I will!"

"Sometimes love isn't enough, Mrs. O'Keefe. Raising a child is more than providing food and shelter. It sickens me to see children allowed to run wild and get into every kind of hazard. The world is a dangerous place."

"But sure, and don't you think I know that? And what makes you such an expert, Sheriff?" Maggie wanted to slap him. She didn't know when she'd been so angry.

He thrust his hands in his pockets. "My mother runs an orphanage for abused children. Believe me, I've seen things that would make that red hair of yours stand on end."

Maggie didn't doubt it. She had seen some things in Chicago that had appalled her. But she wasn't like that. She opened her mouth to explain herself again, then realized arguing with the man was not helping them find Fiona. And night was coming on. Terror seized her again.

"This lollygagging does my Fiona no good." She turned and stalked toward the gathering shadows. She was shaking with rage. She did the best she could with Fiona. What more could she do? She had to make a living, or they would both starve.

Sheriff Masters fell into step beside her. "I'll gather some volunteers."

Maggie could tell by his tone that he still held her in disdain. If she could, she would tell him to take his suspicious face somewhere else, but Fiona needed him. Inclining her head in silent acquiescence, she allowed him to walk beside her. They walked up Miami Street to Hill Street. Sheriff Masters stopped everyone he met and asked for help. Soon an army of more than twenty people was fanning out across the streets of Wabash.

Maggie took hope with her as she poked in bushes and crossed fencerows. Hope sustained her as she peered in the dusty windows of sheds and called Fiona's name in barns where the dust motes danced, but no little girl whirled in delight with them.

By eleven the hunt was called off for the night. Maggie knew it was useless to hunt at night, but the thought of Fiona alone and lost in the dark tormented her. She felt as if the life were being squeezed from her lungs, and despair darkened her thoughts. She couldn't give up. As the townspeople dispersed to their homes and beds, she wandered the streets calling Fiona's name. Desperation drove her, but it was useless. Fiona was gone.

Her muscles ached, and scratches stung her hands where she poked in brambles. It was pitch black and hard to see more than inches in front of her face. She had no idea what time it was, but she kept straining her ears to hear Fiona's childish voice. The only sounds she heard were the lapping of the gurgle from the Wabash River and the distant tinkle of the piano at the bar in town.

Groping through the dark, she found her way to a barn on the outskirts of town and sank down into a soft bed of hay. She would rest a moment before resuming the search. Her eyelids dropped with weariness, and she sighed and drifted into sleep.

When Maggie awoke, she felt as though a thousand needles were stabbing her, but it was only hay. Dawn rimmed the clouds with red, and Maggie stood to her feet. Her throat was raw with shouting for Fiona, and she felt as if her tongue were stuck to the roof of her mouth.

The farmhouse, a modest two-story with a wide front porch, overlooked the Wabash River. A welcoming lamp glowed from one window, and Maggie, shivering in the cool air, made her way across the dew-drenched grass to the porch to ask if she might have some water from the pump.

The door swung open at her first knock. A young woman about Maggie's age peered around the edge of the door, her wide blue eyes as startled as a doe in hunting season. Her unbound hair cascaded down the back of her white nightdress in a glorious profusion of golden curls.

"It's sorry I am to be disturbing you at such an early hour," Maggie stammered. "But have you been seeing a little girl with red hair? Three years old, she is."

"Oh," the woman said in a throaty voice that enveloped Maggie like a hug. "You poor dear. You look exhausted. Have you been searching all night?" She opened the door wider and took Maggie's arm. "Come in and have a cup of tea and some breakfast."

At the kind words Maggie burst into tears and found herself held against the soft cotton nightdress that smelled of sunshine and lemon. The young woman made soothing sounds and patted Maggie on the back. Maggie sobbed out her terror and fear until nothing was left but hiccups and hot, dry eyes. She allowed herself to be led to the kitchen, where she found a young man seated at the table.

He looked up, his eyes registering his alarm. Maggie knew she must look a sight. Her hair had come out of its neat roll on the back of her head, and she could feel wisps of straw still prickling her. She pushed the curls out of her face and gave him a tentative smile.

"This is my husband, Willard. I'm Margaret—Margaret Thomas." She pulled out a chair and gave Maggie a gentle push onto the seat. Her husband, slim with light brown hair and blue eyes, sat at the table. Dressed in dungarees with suspenders over an undershirt, his red flannel shirt lay draped over the back of his chair ready to be donned for the day's work.

Maggie nodded to Willard. It felt good to sit down. It felt even better to have someone worrying about her. Maggie hadn't had that since her mother died. Fresh tears prickled her eyes. Her mother had entrusted Fiona to her and look what had happened. She wasn't fit to raise her sister. She'd let her own excitement about her new business cause her to focus on the work instead of on Fiona.

A neighbor with a small son had offered to keep Fiona during the day for a small sum, but Maggie hadn't thought it necessary. As a laundress at Fort Laramie, Maggie had trained Fiona to stay close. Now Maggie would give not only that modest payment to the neighbor but her whole year's wages to have made a different choice.

She raised a cup of tea wearily to her lips. The hot liquid slid down her parched throat and brought soothing relief to Maggie's spirit. Her gaze wandered around the room. The kitchen window faced the east, and golden sunshine poured through the blue gingham curtains onto the unvarnished wooden floor and transformed the plain room into a place of welcoming warmth. Everything was neat and tidy. Maggie felt more at home than she had since she and her family left Ireland.

She smiled at Margaret. "But sure, and you must be an angel sent from heaven."

Margaret laughed. "Ask Willard—I think he might disagree with that."

"She's an angel with a temper." Willard smiled and looked at his wife, a twinkle in his eyes. "Now tell us why you're wandering around our farm at such an hour." He said the words as if he really cared.

Maggie explained about her missing sister. Her fear and worry, how she had been too busy to make friends in town, the way she felt alone since her parents died. As she talked, Margaret and Willard nodded sympathetically, and Maggie's tongue loosened even more. The loneliness she'd held inside flooded out as she realized these two could be her friends. She was almost afraid to believe it.

Margaret insisted she eat some toast and a poached egg. It was pure ambrosia to Maggie. When had she eaten last? She thought back. Breakfast yesterday morning, surely. Toast and tea. She'd been too busy to eat lunch and had only fixed jam and toast for Fiona. Shame washed over her. The sheriff was right. She didn't deserve Fiona. A bakery with luscious food, and all she took time to fix her beloved sister was jam and toast. She would do better when Fiona was found. And she *would* be found. Maggie refused to consider any other option.

"The sheriff thinks I was negligent," Maggie said in a tortured voice. Just saying the words made her shudder. Her eyes stung with tears of self-reproach.

Margaret leaned forward and took her hand, then squeezed it gently. "You haven't lived here long enough to know much about the people. Simon's father was a drunk who used poor Simon and his sister as drudges. I went to school with Simon. More than once I saw him come in with a shiner or covered with bruises. Most days they came with nothing for lunch." She glanced tenderly at her husband. "I fell in love with Willard in the fifth grade when he gave Simon his lunch. Willard almost always brought extra to try to feed Simon. Now our sheriff tries to help other kids who are in the same plight he was. When his father died, his mother married a wonderful man. Now that he's gone, Abigail uses the money he left to care for abused and orphaned children."

She released Maggie's hand and stood. "But you've never abused Fiona. I can tell that from talking with you. I'll talk to Simon. He has a good heart. You'll see."

Maggie was certain that Sheriff Masters didn't like her. She could sense it. And she had a feeling it had nothing to do with her fitness to raise Fiona. "Um, one more thing," she said hesitantly. "He thinks Fiona is me own daughter. 'Tis sure if he finds out she's only me sister, he'll take her from me."

Margaret's eyes widened. "I can't lie to him, Maggie."

"I didn't lie to him, either. 'Tis his own jumping to conclusions that made him think Fiona was me own wee one. But sure, and can't we let him continue in his error?" Maggie clutched Margaret's hand in desperation.

Margaret looked to Willard, who shrugged. "If he asks us, we'll have to tell him the truth," she warned. "An omission is still a lie when you know you should correct it."

That would have to do. Maggie nodded. " 'Tis thankful I am to have found you. I'll prove to the sheriff that I'm fit to care for Fiona. Then I'll be telling him the truth meself."

Margaret nodded, but Maggie could tell she still didn't like it. And Maggie didn't like it, either. Her mother had always raised her to know that a person's word was all they had in the end. Integrity was everything. But once Fiona was safely home, she would show the sheriff what a good mother she was. Then it wouldn't matter. She was sure of that.

She tried to tell herself she hadn't lied, not really. But why did her stomach tighten at the thought? Why did she feel God would not bless her deception? For Maggie feared the God of anger her mother had told her about. She gritted her teeth and stood. She would even risk God's wrath for her sister. Following Willard and Margaret to town, she vowed to make it up to Fiona. Then she would worry about what the sheriff thought.

She spotted the sheriff standing with a group of people

in front of the courthouse. He stood head and shoulders above the rest, his uniform in striking contrast to the dungarees and work shirts of the men. He turned his head, and his gaze caught hers. Was that censure in his stare? Maggie thought it was, and a knot formed in her stomach.

Sheriff Masters held up his hands. "Here's Mrs. O'Keefe now. Any sign of Fiona?" he asked.

Maggie shook her head. "Me poor, wee girl. Please, we have to find her." Her voice was reedy with despair. She'd clung to the hope that someone had found Fiona in the night. Where could she be? She refused to let her mind dwell on the dangers held in the area.

As the day dragged on, it was all Maggie could do to hold onto her hope. Her life would be worth nothing without her sister. She was the reason Maggie worked so hard, why she'd given up her job as a laundress at the fort for the chance at something better. It was for Fiona, always for Fiona. The thought that she might never see that bright smile or feel Fiona's small arms around her neck nearly drove Maggie insane. Was she hungry and scared? Her breath came in short gasps. She had to find her sister.

two

Two days with no sign of Fiona. Simon Masters pushed his hat to the back of his head and wiped his forehead with his handkerchief. The sun beat down in a sweltering haze of humidity, an unusually hot day for March. If the little girl was out in this heat with no food or water, he feared they would not find her alive. He and the child's mother had poked into every berry bush, every crevice. Now they walked the length of the Wabash-Erie Canal. The muddy water held bits of clothing, sticks, and leaves, but no trace of Fiona. For that he was grateful.

He cast a sidelong glance at Maggie O'Keefe. Her dark green eyes stared out of her white face. He had no doubt she loved her daughter. But he'd seen too much to believe that love was enough. He still carried the scars on his back from a man who claimed to love him. He intended to think carefully before making a decision about Fiona. The law didn't protect these young ones enough, in Simon's mind. But he had the power to enforce the meager laws on the books.

The young woman sat on a rock at the canal's edge. "You think she's dead, don't you?" The words were quiet but held a wealth of pain and grief.

Simon didn't want to answer that question. He didn't even want to examine it in his own heart. Finding young Timmy McDougal had almost torn him apart with grief.

His responsibilities weighed heavily upon him. "Tomorrow is Sunday. I've asked all the churches in town to announce her disappearance. Maybe someone has taken her in."

Her eyes widened, and hope tinged her pale cheeks with color. "You really think so? I can't bear the thought that she might be hungry and scared." Her voice was full of misery.

"We've certainly found no trace of her." He handed her his canteen, and she took the cap off and gulped a mouthful of water.

Grimacing, she handed it back. "Margaret is bringing lunch to all the searchers. We'd better get over to the church."

He nodded and held out his hand to help her to her feet. Her fingers closed around his. They were rough and calloused with work. Simon felt a stab of pity. What had brought her to Wabash? Alone and with a child to support—yet she'd squared her shoulders and set to work. He pushed the questions away. It was really none of his business. Maggie wouldn't welcome his nosiness. She already held him at arm's length for his censorship of the care she'd given her daughter. But he was a self-proclaimed advocate of abused children. He'd seen what fine and upstanding people could do to children, and he'd learned to look beyond the surface. Time would tell what kind of care Fiona had received from her mother.

When he took this job, no one said it would be easy. Laws had been written to protect children, even more as 1870 neared. Since the War Between the States, the nation was moving forward, more aware of those less fortunate than before. Orphanages like his mother's were needed in the wake of the war.

They walked in silence up Miami Street toward the church. Already he could see people milling in front of the church house. A woman separated from the crowd and ran toward them.

"She's been found!" Margaret's cheeks were flushed with excitement.

Maggie's face went even whiter, and she clutched Margaret's arm. "Where is she? Is she all right?"

"She'll be fine. The Bickwells found her in their wagon when they got out to their farm."

"Why didn't they bring her back right away?" Simon frowned and glanced around for Fiona. His sister knew better than to keep a child from her mother.

"She's sick, and they didn't think she should be moved right now." Margaret linked arms with Maggie.

"Everett could have come back with word so we weren't still searching." Simon intended to speak to them about their negligence in reporting Fiona's safe recovery.

Maggie stopped and turned eyes full of worry to Margaret. "She's sick? 'Tis sure I must go to her right away! Where are these Bickwells?" She said the name awkwardly.

"About four miles out of town. Leora is my sister. She and Everett have a large milking operation. She loves kids." Indeed she was almost obsessed with them. Married ten years, the couple had never had children of their own. "Mother tried to get them to adopt one of her little waifs, but Leora insisted she wanted her own child."

"Leora is your sister?"

Simon nodded. "She'll take very good care of Fiona, I promise you. Leora sometimes teaches the Miami Indian children in the area, and Everett preaches out at the Meshingomesia Miami Indian reserve on Sundays. She'll love the opportunity to lavish attention on Fiona. Let me rustle up a buggy, and I'll take you to see her."

Maggie nodded hesitantly and pressed her lips together, a look of caution in her eyes. Simon couldn't blame her. She regarded him as the enemy and probably thought his sister would be no better. He hurried down the boardwalk to the stable and rented a buggy. Hitching the horse to the buggy, he found himself wishing he could bring a smile to Maggie's somber face. With its light dusting of freckles and those green eyes that tilted up at the corners, it was a face that was made for laughter, not tears. But he suspected Maggie O'Keefe had experienced more than her share of sorrow.

She barely waited for him to bring the buggy to a halt before she gathered her skirts and clambered up beside him. She sat on the edge of her seat staring forward as though her posture could get them to Fiona more quickly.

The buggy wheels clattered over the new corduroy road that connected Wabash and Marion. It was too noisy for much social talk, so the trip was made mostly in silence, broken only twice when Maggie asked how much farther it would be. They passed through Treaty, then turned west down the muddy track that led to his sister's farm.

It had been nearly a month since Simon had made a trip out here. He loved his sister, but sometimes she got on his nerves. He didn't understand the way she seemed to think her entire happiness was wrapped up in having a child. No matter what they talked about, she managed to turn the conversation to children. Simon loved kids, but he wouldn't shrivel and die if he never had a son.

Leora's flower bulbs were beginning to come up, and the splash of color brightened the rest of the small yard. He helped Maggie down, then led her to the door. His rap on the door was answered almost immediately. Leora was dressed in a blue cotton gown with a large white apron swathing her slim figure.

She gave a cry of delight. "Simon!" Her inquisitive gaze went to Maggie.

Simon could tell by the look on his sister's face that she thought Maggie was someone he was courting. He hastened to dispel that notion. "Leora, this is Fiona's mother, Maggie."

Leora stepped back inside the door, and her expression darkened. "I told Everett to tell you she couldn't be moved."

Simon was taken aback at her protective stance. He glanced at Maggie and saw his own confusion mirrored on her face. "He told us," he said. "Maggie wanted to see Fiona and make sure she was all right."

Leora opened the door, but Simon could see her obvious reluctance. "She's in the room at the end of the hall."

Maggie brushed past her, but Leora followed closely behind. They reminded Simon of two hens laying claim to the same chick. A sense of foreboding gripped him. Had Maggie neglected Fiona more than he had suspected? He pushed the thought away. Her concern was so obvious that he found it hard to believe she would hurt her daughter.

By the time he reached the bedroom, Maggie had thrown herself down beside Fiona. The child was covered with bruises, and a deep gash marred her forehead. The little girl's face was flushed, but she gave a cry of delight and wrapped skinny arms around Maggie's neck.

"You was gone," she said in a small voice full of reproach. "I called and called, but I couldn't find you."

"But sure, and you frightened me half to death," Maggie said. "You know better than to wander off."

"The kitten ran away from me," Fiona said. "Then I fell in the canal."

Maggie gasped and clutched Fiona more tightly. "I've told you never to go near the canal." Her face was wet with tears.

"I'm sorry," Fiona said. She patted Maggie's wet face with her small hands.

"She's been asking for Maggie," Leora put in. "She says Maggie is her sister."

Simon's gaze shot to Maggie's face. The color drained out of her face, and she opened her mouth, but no sound emerged. She pursed her lips and shot a pleading glance at Simon. He stared back, still confused.

"I–I *am* her sister," Maggie whispered.

An expression of triumph crossed Leora's face. "So you say. Where are her mother and father?"

" 'Tis these three years since they died," Maggie said. "Fiona and me alone are left. Fa died in a train accident, and me mother soon followed him when Fiona was but a week old."

Leora nodded and turned to Simon. "Then I think you should investigate the care she is providing for Fiona, Simon. Everett and I shall ask the judge to award temporary custody of Fiona to us. We can provide a good, stable home for the child. Maggie is scarcely more than a child herself."

" 'Tis no child I am! But sure, and I'm nearly eighteen meself," Maggie said. "How can any judge rip me sister away from me? I'm the only mama she has ever known! You would rip a babe from her mother?" Her voice shook with the intensity of her emotion.

Simon's heart sank. This was turning into more of a problem than he'd thought. "You lied to me," he said slowly. He wasn't sure why that realization stung so much. And she was a minor as well.

"Never did I lie! You assumed, and I never corrected you." Maggie put her hands on her hips and glared at him. " 'Tis sure I was that you would take the same attitude I see in your face."

She was right. He *had* assumed she was the child's mother. His outrage abated a bit, but the circumstances remained the same. He would have to delve into the problem further. Just what he didn't want to do. And he was caught between his sister and the law.

He gave a heavy sigh. "We'll see what the judge says," he said slowly. "But I'll not take her from her home, Leora, just to fill your empty arms."

Leora flushed and looked away. Her lips tightened. "We'll see what the judge says."

"We'd better go," Simon said. This could get tricky. Under normal circumstances a judge would likely see that Maggie had performed admirably in raising her sister, but the whole town had been mobilized over this incident. And the judge was Everett's cousin.

Fresh tears swam in Maggie's eyes, turning them into liquid pools of emerald, and fresh pity stabbed Simon. This was a part of his job he didn't enjoy. He reached out to Maggie, offering his assistance.

He could see the emotions warring for control in her face. Rebellion, anger, resignation. She looked down at her sister, then leaned over and pressed a kiss to Fiona's forehead. "Rest easy, Darlin'. I'll be back to see you soon. No one will keep us apart."

Fiona's lips drew up in a pout. "I want to come home, Maggie." She wailed when Leora settled her back against the pillows.

Leora soothed her, and Simon pulled Maggie toward the door. She left with a strange resignation on her face, and Simon could tell she hardly knew what she was doing. But what else could he do? He couldn't let a minor take charge of the child when the circumstances were so dim and uncertain. Much as he hated to admit it, his sister had a point. The child hardly looked like a well-cared-for little girl.

He led Maggie through the house and out the door. As he helped her into the buggy, she resisted for a moment, then sighed and allowed him to assist her. Her hands were fisted into her lap, and her eyes were wide and unseeing as he pulled out of the yard.

As they turned onto the main road back to town, she gave a sob. "If your sister wants a child so badly, why doesn't she get one from your mother's orphanage? 'Tis not right that she should take me sister from me."

"I've encouraged her to do that. But she says she wants her own child. I've never seen her take to a child the way she has to Fiona." And Fiona was an engaging child, even Simon could see that. She was a small version of Maggie.

" 'Tis not my fault. She does not belong with your Leora. Your sister cannot steal someone else's child to ease her own pain. 'Tis not right."

He didn't answer. What could he say? He hated the thought of bringing more pain to Maggie, but he feared it was about to come upon her head. Judge Thompson and Everett were cousins, though as close as brothers. He would likely do whatever they asked. And maybe they were right. Fiona seemed pretty battered. How did he know it had all happened while she was missing? And she had fallen in the canal! Only God's grace kept the little girl from drowning, certainly not Maggie's care.

Simon resolved to ask his mother's opinion of this. Maybe she could persuade Leora to hold off until he determined the right thing to do. Yes, Maggie had not exercised proper supervision over Fiona, but any child could slip away when a mother's back was turned. He was not at all convinced yet that she was unfit as a mother for Fiona. He turned over in his mind ideas of ways to prove to himself and to Leora whether Maggie was fit to care for Fiona, but nothing came to him.

It was nearly dark when he pulled up outside Maggie's home, though the full moon illuminated the yard nearly as well as a lantern. The house was dark and unfriendly. Simon helped her down. "Let me light a lantern for you," he said.

" 'Tis not a bother for me to do it," Maggie said. "But sure, and I am used to taking care of meself and Fiona."

He walked her to the door. "I'm sorry, Maggie."

"Don't be sorry. But sure, and the war's not over. I'll not lose me sister. No one can take her from me." Her words were assured, but there was no hiding the haunted expression in her eyes.

A sudden impulse struck him. "Do you attend church anywhere? My mother would be honored if you would join us for the church dinner on Saturday."

Maggie gasped. "You take me sister from our home, then invite me to church? What kind of monster are you, Sheriff? 'Tis sure I'm not impressed with your piety when you can tear a little girl from her own home and from the one who loves her." Her back stiff, she pushed open the door and stepped inside. "I'll not attend your church to free your guilt." She shut the door firmly in Simon's face.

He felt as though he'd just fought a battle. And lost. She had a point. What had possessed him to try to socialize with her? He needed to keep his mind on his job. Getting personally involved would muddy the waters. Maggie needed help, but he wasn't the one to give it to her.

Simon climbed back into the buggy and guided it up the hill to the stable. He walked down Wabash Street to his room over his office. Maybe he needed legal counsel about what to do. His lawyer friend was out of town, but Simon resolved to ask his opinion on the matter as soon as he returned. Simon wanted to do the right thing. But he wasn't sure what that was.

three

The sunshine streaming through the bedroom window woke Maggie, and she bolted upright in the bed. She should have been at the stove hours ago! Three nights without sleep had taken its toll. Tossing aside the bedding, she leapt out of bed and dressed quickly. Baking was the last thing she felt like doing. She wanted to get a buggy and go out and take Fiona from the proud woman who had kidnapped her. For that's what it felt like, a kidnapping, pure and simple.

She had known it wasn't safe to let the sheriff know she wasn't Fiona's mother. That was precisely why they had come to Wabash. The authorities in Chicago had tried to separate them, and Maggie had taken Fiona and run as far and as fast as she could. From the looks of things, it hadn't been far enough or fast enough.

For awhile she had thought the sheriff might be an ally, but in spite of his displeasure at his sister's tactics, he had upheld what she was doing. Maggie despised the law. What good was it to her? The sheriff came into her shop wearing that silver star, giving her the impression he was a friend. But he was a foe, like every other lawman she'd come in contact with. Law existed only for the upright, the church-going. Not for poor Irish scum.

Her shoulders slumped in defeat, Maggie scurried down the steps and threw kindling into the cookstove.

Once the flame had been coaxed to burn, she added some corncobs and shut the door. While the fire got good and hot, she would mix up the first batch of bread. The customers would be sorely disappointed not to find fresh bakery items until later in the morning, but there was no help for it.

The bell on the front door tinkled, and Maggie poked her head into the display room. Her heart sank when she saw Sheriff Masters's broad shoulders. Smoothing her hair, she stepped into the room. "I'd hoped not to see the likes of you this day," she said with a toss of her head.

His tentative smile faltered. "My mother asked me to stop by for some bread."

She couldn't afford to turn down any sale, even if it was to the enemy. "All I have was made two days ago."

"That's fine. I'll take three loaves."

Silently Maggie wrapped his bread in paper and handed it to him, then put his money in her cash box.

He cleared his throat. "Judge Thompson is hearing the case tomorrow at two. You'll need to be there."

Fresh rage swept over Maggie, and she wanted to beat against his chest with her fists. It was only with the greatest effort she managed to control herself. "But sure, and I'll be there. Your family will not take me sister from me. We belong together!"

"The court will decide that. I'm not denying you love Fiona. But sometimes love isn't enough. I'm sure you want what's best for her."

"You will force me to go to court?" Maggie felt like crying, but she raised her chin defiantly. He would not cow her. None of them would. She would find a way to keep Fiona.

"I have no choice. The law is clear. You are both minors."

" 'Tis true, but me sister is no trouble. I'm the only mum she knows."

"How was that allowed to happen? Surely the authorities should have been concerned before now."

Heat rose up Maggie's neck, and she looked away. She could sense the sheriff's gaze on her, and she forced herself to meet his stare. His eyes were a warm brown, the reddish brown of the buckeyes that fell from the tree outside her back door. He did seem to care. Maggie wondered about that.

She cleared her throat. " 'Tis true there was some talk of putting us in an orphanage," she admitted. She would not tell him of the places she'd worked as maid or housekeeper all over Illinois and Indiana. His eyes were too keen.

The sheriff's eyes softened. "Perhaps this is for the best then. Once you reach your majority, you can get Fiona back. I'll make sure you're allowed to visit often."

A lump grew in Maggie's throat, and she blinked furiously at the tears that pricked her eyes. "I can't lose me sister," she whispered. "Me fa and mum would not rest easy in their graves if I allowed that to happen. She is all I have left." She didn't want to admit that to him, but the words seemed wrung from her.

"I'm afraid you have no choice, Miss O'Keefe." The sheriff tucked the bread under his arm and slapped the hat back on his head. Nodding to her, he went to the door. "Don't forget—tomorrow at two." The doorbell tinkled again as he left.

Maggie leaned weakly against the display case. Her

throat closed with tears, and she wept. What was she to do? What was the right thing to do? Maybe she had deprived Fiona of a normal life by dragging her from pillar to post over the past three years, but she and Fiona loved each other. They belonged together.

It made Maggie tired trying to think of what to do. She wished she could crawl back in bed and pull the quilt over her head. But she couldn't do that. Fiona was depending on her. Every day the odds seemed to mount against them. For awhile it appeared things might work out for them here in Wabash. Now that hope was dwindling fast. Maggie sighed and pushed the thoughts away. She had work to do, and maybe if she stayed busy, she could keep the fear at bay.

She spent the day baking and tending to customers. Some of them looked at her strangely when they came in, and she knew they had heard the rumors that she was unfit to care for her sister, that the sheriff's own sister was taking her before a judge. Let them stare! She would hold her head up, and she would get her sister back. The gossipmongers. As if they cared for Fiona's welfare, a one of them!

The next day Maggie felt as though ants were crawling over her skin. She was jumpy, and her heart pounded every time the bakery door opened. For the umpteenth time she checked the watch pinned to her dress and took a deep breath. Fifteen minutes until the court met. She needed to leave now.

She took off her apron and checked to make sure her hair was in place. It wouldn't do to look less than competent. Locking the door behind her, Maggie walked to the courthouse. She saw Fiona with Leora and Everett.

Leora wouldn't look at Maggie, though Maggie tried to catch her eye. She wanted to plead with the woman not to do this thing.

Fiona saw her and jerked her hand from Leora's. "Maggie!" She scrambled across the yard to Maggie.

Maggie swept her up in her arms and buried her face in her sweet-smelling hair. It felt so good to hold her.

"Please give her to me." Leora's voice was tight with suppressed anger. "She is in my care for now."

Maggie stared her down. "But sure, and I'll carry her in. The judge hasn't ruled yet. Until then me sister belongs with me."

Leora's expression darkened. She opened her mouth, but her husband put a restraining hand on her arm. "Leave it be."

Leora's eyes filled with tears, and she jerked her arm away from her husband. His tender expression was replaced with resignation. "Come along, Darling. The judge will be waiting."

Leora marched ahead of him, every stiff line of her back proclaiming her outrage. Maggie clutched Fiona to her chest and started toward the courthouse. Everett offered her the support of his arm, but she shook her head.

The courthouse was a dilapidated building that had been a barracks. It smelled of sweat and decay. Maggie followed Everett and Leora into the courtroom and sank into a hard-backed chair with Fiona still in her arms. Sheriff Masters was already in the room. He turned and nodded to her. His sister sat in the chair beside him and leaned over to whisper to him. He nodded occasionally, but when he whispered back to Leora, she jerked away and folded her arms across her chest.

"All rise," the bailiff declared.

Maggie struggled to her feet as he announced the judge's entrance.

Judge Thompson was younger than she expected. He looked to be in his mid-thirties with thick black hair and piercing blue eyes. He sat at the bench and shuffled the papers in front of him. Leaning back in his chair, he crossed his arms over his chest. "Let's dispense with formalities. Tell me what's going on. I'll hear from you first, Sheriff."

Sheriff Masters rose and approached the bench. "Do you want to swear me in?"

Judge Thompson shook his head. "We've known each other a long time, Simon. You won't lie to me. Just tell me the situation."

The sheriff nodded. "We have here Fiona O'Keefe. She's been in the care of her seventeen-year-old sister for the past three years."

Judge Thompson held up his hand. "Do you mean to tell me this young woman has been caring for her since she was fourteen?"

Sheriff Masters nodded.

The judge grunted. "Continue."

"Fiona wandered away after being left unattended in the backyard. She was missing for two days. We later learned that Everett Bickwell found her in his wagon. He and Leora are asking for temporary custody of the child, citing the sister's age and inability to care properly for the child."

Maggie wanted to jump to her feet and say it wasn't like that. She was quite competent to care for her sister. And Fiona had never wandered away before. But the words stuck in her throat when the judge turned his piercing eyes on her.

"Well, speak up, young woman. What do you have to say for yourself?" The judge's voice was kind in spite of his words.

Maggie stood on shaky legs and forced herself to approach the judge. She feared her knees wouldn't hold her. " 'Tis true, Sir. Me sister and I have been on our own since she was a wee babe of only one week. But me Fiona is all I have in the world, and I'm all she has. Me business is doing well, and I make sure she is well fed and cared for. As for her wandering away, any bairn is apt to do that. Me Fiona knows better, and she won't do it again—isn't that right, Fiona?"

Her sister, still cradled against Maggie's chest, nodded. She wound her skinny arms around Maggie's neck in a choking hold. "I want to stay with Maggie."

The judge rested his chin on his hand and sighed. "What do you have to say, Leora? Knowing you, I'm sure it's all you could do to keep quiet."

Simon chuckled, and Leora shot him an angry glance. She rose and approached the bench with a deliberate pace. "When Everett brought Fiona to me, she was in a dreadful state, Mason."

She was calling the judge by his first name. Maggie's heart sank. They must know one another. What did she expect in this town?

Leora continued. "Bruises all over her—filthy. Obviously Miss O'Keefe was neglecting her far more than she would have you believe."

Maggie gasped and opened her mouth to refute the lies, but Leora rolled right over Maggie's indignation.

"And the burden of a child at her age is too much for any young woman. Everett and I are prepared to offer the child a permanent home, but we are willing to accept temporary custody until the court decides on the proper course of action."

A permanent home? Confusion clouded Maggie's thinking and slowed her responses. This couldn't be happening! Clutching Fiona tighter, she forced her words out. "Never have I mistreated me sister! If she had bruises or cuts, it was from falling in the canal!" Too late she realized the danger of her words. She felt sick at Leora's expression of triumph.

"Exactly my point, Mason! The child fell in the canal. It was only by God's grace that she didn't drown, certainly not by any quality of care offered by her sister."

The judge sighed. "What is your opinion, Simon?"

Maggie turned to look at the sheriff. His steady gaze didn't waver.

"I wish I could tell you with certainty. Certainly Miss O'Keefe is to be commended for caring for her sister these past three years. And I'm sure she will keep a closer eye on the child. My inclination is that you award her custody of her sister, under the court's supervision. I know she is a minor, but she has lived and worked on her own for several years. I am willing to check in on her and the child at the court's discretion."

Leora drew in a sharp gasp of outrage, and Maggie did the same. Supervision? She didn't need supervision. But at least the sheriff wasn't totally against her. She fixed her gaze on the judge.

He sighed. "What a pickle we have here. But I think the law is clear. Miss O'Keefe is a minor. We can't have a minor in charge of another minor. You win, Leora. But only until I have a chance to think about this situation. We'll revisit the permanent custody matter in two months. We will decide on permanent custody at that time." He fixed his gaze on Maggie.

"I'll be eighteen by then, your honor," Maggie said.

"But still a minor, Miss. We will take this all under advisement."

Two months without her sister. How could she bear it? Maggie struggled to hold back the tears.

The judge slammed the gavel. "So ordered. We will revisit the issue of permanent custody at that time."

Permanent custody? Maggie's thoughts were in a whirl as Leora pulled a wailing Fiona from her arms and carried her out like a contender carrying a trophy. Maggie wanted to hurt someone, and the sheriff was closest. She flew at him like an avenging angel and beat against his chest with her fists.

"This is all your fault," she sobbed. "Me sister will pine without me."

Sheriff Masters let her pound at him, then seized her wrists in a gentle but firm grasp. "I'm sorry, Miss O'Keefe. I know this is hard for you. But it's not forever. Permanent custody won't be set for another two months. We'll talk to the judge again then."

"What good will that do?" she wailed. "Your sister will never give her up." She jerked out of his grasp and ran to the door. Pulling it open, she ran from the room as though a thousand demons chased her. Demons she thought she had outrun long ago.

four

Simon felt like a traitor. He wished he could have done something, but it was taken out of his hands. Pity welled in his heart for Maggie. What would she do now? He'd never seen such desperation on a face before. He would have to keep an eye on her. She might try something stupid. Like taking Fiona and running.

He chatted with Judge Thompson a few minutes, then shook his hand and strode out of the courtroom. He made his way down to Maggie's bakery and opened the door. He could hear muffled sobs from the back room. The sobs were accompanied by banging. "Miss O'Keefe?" he called. There was no response. She likely couldn't hear him for the commotion she was making. Simon pushed open the door to the back room and stepped through.

Maggie was sobbing as she thrust clothes and other belongings into a trunk by the back door. Packing. He was right to be uneasy about her intentions. He cleared his throat, and she whirled around, nearly tumbling to the floor in her shock.

"But sure, and you've come to see me misery!" she cried. " 'Tis all your fault! You and that hoity-toity sister of yours. If you'd made her give me Fiona when we found her, none of this would have happened."

"No, you would have taken her and escaped into the night—isn't that right?" he asked quietly.

"Yes, I would have!" She rose and put her fists on her hips.

Simon was touched by her defiance. She was a woman who loved deeply. Some man would have a loyal and devoted wife someday. He frowned. Where had that thought come from? "What are you doing, Miss O'Keefe?"

"But sure, and you're a smart one, Sheriff. You tell me!" The defiance drained from her face, and she sat on the edge of the trunk.

"You're planning on snatching Fiona and running away."

Two spots of red bloomed in her white cheeks. "But sure, and can you blame me? Me and Fiona belong together! No law can keep us apart."

"That won't solve anything, Miss O'Keefe. I would have to find you and bring Fiona back."

"Just let me go, Sheriff. Give me a few hours' head start, and you'll never see either of us again. I'll take good care of Fiona—I promise."

Her pleading broke Simon's heart. He wished he could grant her request. But he'd sworn to uphold the law, and that's exactly what he would have to do. "I'm sorry," he said softly.

Maggie's shoulders slumped, and she buried her face in her hands and wept. Simon knelt beside her and put an arm around her shoulders. She felt so small and fragile as she turned and buried her face in his chest. She just fit there. Her hair smelled sweetly of cinnamon and sugar. Simon shivered, then pulled away. What was he thinking? He didn't have any business comforting her. She was considering committing a crime.

Maggie gave a little hiccup and wiped the back of her

hand over her eyes. "What are you going to do?" Her voice was small and resigned.

"Nothing."

She jerked her head up and stared at him. He grinned at her. "It's not a crime to *think* about something. Just make sure you don't do it."

Her reddened eyes blinked in surprise, and she smiled back. It was the first time he'd ever seen her smile. The dimple in her left cheek gave her an impish look. He stepped away, at a loss to understand why he was so drawn to her. Young women more lovely than she had tried to catch his eye. But for some reason Maggie drew him in a way he'd never experienced. He wasn't sure he liked the sensation.

Her dimple deepened. "But sure, and you'd better be getting out there catching the criminals."

"I'd much rather talk to you," he admitted. He would have taken back the words if he could. This was dangerous ground.

She looked startled; then a blush swept over her cheeks. "Why did you come back here?"

"I wanted to check on you." He bit back the real reasons. Reasons he had no business thinking. From the first moment he met her, she was never far from his thoughts. Such an admission would likely frighten her.

She nodded. "But sure, and I'd better be getting back to me work."

It was only as he was striding up Miami Street toward his mother's that he realized she hadn't promised not to try to snatch Fiona and run.

❧

As soon as she heard the front door close, Maggie flew

into action again. She had a plan, and not even the sheriff's handsome face could sway her from it. A twinge of guilt broke her concentration, but she pushed it away. She had no choice. No court, no judge could tell her Fiona didn't belong to her. She would keep her things packed, then grab Fiona at the most opportune time. The sheriff may have thought he had stopped her plan, but he would soon find out differently. Telling herself to have patience, she put the last of her dresses in the trunk and closed the lid.

She'd seen a notice at the post office about a dinner being held tonight at the church on Hill Street. It was the church the sheriff attended, so she assumed his entire family went there also. She could only hope Leora would bring her new "daughter" to show her off. Maggie ground her teeth together at the thought of the sheriff's sister. A thief, that's all she was. Just because she couldn't have children of her own gave her no right to steal someone else's family.

The delicious aroma of cinnamon rolls wafted through the kitchen. She would take some of her prized rolls to the dinner. It was too bad she would have to use the sheriff's invitation in such a manner, but it couldn't be helped. She would tell him she'd thought better of her refusal to come. Guilt nibbled at her, but she wouldn't let it change her mind.

She iced the rolls, put them on a rack to cool, then grabbed a shawl and hurried to the door. Turning the *Closed* side of the sign around, she strolled to the canal boat depot. The sheriff would likely expect her to take the train out of town. When he discovered she was missing, she hoped he wouldn't think about the canal. Not many people traveled by canal anymore. It was slow and dreary compared to the speed and efficiency of the train.

She bought two tickets from an old man who looked more dead than alive. He showed no interest in her or her plans. She was glad the tickets were cheap. Hurrying back home, she flipped the *Closed* sign around to *Open* and went to the back kitchen. She laid out the clothes they would wear. She would dress in one of Fa's shirts and pants. It would be for the best. No one would think to check for a young man and his daughter traveling by canal boat. She would have to cut her hair. The thought gripped her with dismay. Twirling a curl around her finger, she pushed away the regret. She would have to give up her one vanity, but no sacrifice was too great for her and Fiona to stay together.

At five she put out the CLOSED sign and picked up the basket of cinnamon rolls. Dressed in her best blue dress, she thought no one would suspect she was a woman on a mission. With the basket on her arm, she started up Miami Street hill. An afternoon shower had left the streets a quagmire of mud, and muck soon coated her boots and weighed down her steps.

Her spirits flagged along with her heavy boots. Would this plan even work? Leora would likely watch Fiona like a hawk. Maggie gritted her teeth. It had to work! She would *make* it work. She wished she could pray, but that comfort was denied her. God had ceased to listen to her girlish prayers the week her parents had died. She was no longer sure there even *was* a God.

Squaring her shoulders, she marched to the church door. Almost immediately she saw Margaret and Willard. Margaret saw her at the same time and rushed to enfold

Maggie in a hug.

"I had no idea you were coming," she said. "Willard and I could have stopped to pick you up." She linked arms with Maggie and drew her into a large room filled with people.

Maggie set out her cinnamon rolls to gasps of delight from the people standing near the food table. She overheard one man remark that he would skip the meal and head straight for the dessert to make sure he got some rolls. Her heart lighter, Maggie followed Margaret through the crowd.

"Have you seen Leora Bickwell?" she asked.

Margaret's eyes shadowed with concern. "Not yet. I heard what happened, though. I'm very sorry, Maggie. But take heart—you'll get Fiona back."

"I know. 'Tis patience I must rehearse."

"You mean practice," Margaret said and giggled. "I love that Irish accent! How long since you left Ireland?"

"Me fa brought us over a little over five years ago. Before Fiona was born." Maggie smiled, but her heart sank a little. She'd finally found a friend, one who apparently approved of everything about her, but she would have to leave Margaret behind. Wabash had seemed a place Maggie and Fiona could call home for the rest of their lives. But it was not to be.

Margaret waved. "Simon, look who's here!"

The sheriff's head swivelled at Margaret's call, and Maggie found herself staring at him. She felt a tug toward the sheriff—she couldn't pretend it wasn't so. She wished he felt the same. But all he felt was pity. She'd seen it in his eyes when he held her while she wept.

He was an attractive man with his broad shoulders

and that thick shock of hair. Auburn, it was, though not nearly as red as Maggie's own. But that wasn't what tugged at Maggie. Appearances had never mattered much to her. She saw the kindness in his gaze and the integrity in his face. He was a man who would be a strong ally. And a formidable opponent. She shivered and dropped her gaze. She wished they didn't have to be opponents.

Sheriff Masters came toward them, and Maggie gazed into his eyes as he approached. His smile was welcoming, as if he truly was glad she'd come. Guilt pricked her. He wouldn't look so pleased if he knew her real objective.

"Miss O'Keefe," he said, "you changed your mind."

" 'Tis lonely to sit at home when the whole town is celebrating," she said. "And I'd hoped to see Fiona as well. Has she arrived with Leora?"

The light in his eyes died a bit, and Maggie couldn't help but wonder if he thought she'd come to see him, that she was interested in him. Surely not. He would likely be terrified if he thought she regarded him as more than the town sheriff.

He took her hand and pressed it. "She's not here yet, but I expect them any minute. I'd like you to meet my mother, though."

Maggie smiled in apology at Margaret and allowed Sheriff Masters to lead her through the crowd toward a woman surrounded by children. They ranged in age from infants to young women nearly Maggie's age. The woman herself caught Maggie's gaze. Wings of white softened the glossy black hair she wore in a coronet of braids. Dressed in dark blue, she was an arresting figure.

But what struck Maggie the most was the acceptance and compassion in her gaze as she watched her son bring Maggie toward the group.

She remained seated but held out her hand to Maggie. "You must be Miss O'Keefe. Simon has told me so much about you. You're as lovely as he described."

Maggie nearly gasped aloud but caught herself in time. She slanted a glance at the sheriff. A tide of red was creeping up his neck, and he seemed to avoid Maggie's gaze. Had he really said she was lovely, or was his mother putting words in his mouth?

"Sit by me, Dear. Simon, would you fetch some punch while your Miss O'Keefe and I get acquainted?"

Simon gave Maggie a rueful glance and went off to find the punch. The children scattered as if it had been planned as well. Maggie felt bereft when he left. His mother made her uncomfortable with her direct gaze and even more direct speech. What did she expect from her? She swallowed and clutched her hands together in her lap.

"Don't look so frightened, my dear. I won't bite. You must call me Abigail. I have a feeling we're going to be great friends." Mrs. Masters said the words with utter conviction as though she had determined for it to be so.

"Please call me Maggie." What else could she say? Surely the woman wanted something.

"Of course. Now tell me about yourself."

It was a command, and Maggie found herself doing just that. The older woman's dark gaze, so like her son's, never left Maggie's face. She nodded in sympathy as Maggie told her about the lack of work in Ireland, of how Fa had decided to come to America. She winced when Maggie told her about the train accident and the illness that had carried their mother to her death a week later.

"Well, my dear, you've had a hard life, but I see you're the stronger for it. God must love you very much to hone you at such a young age."

Maggie's eyes widened. "God cares nothing for me. If He even exists."

"Oh, He exists all right, my young friend. And I have a feeling you're about to find that out." Abigail smiled and patted Maggie's arm. "Now I have a proposition for you. My headstrong daughter is determined to keep your sister, but I truly think Fiona belongs with you. In my work I see too many children longing for their own family, their own siblings and parents. We must convince the judge you are a fit guardian for your sister. I'm sure my son has told you I run an orphanage?"

Maggie nodded. "These children are from your orphanage?"

"Yes. But I would like you to become a resident. Then we can petition the judge to give Fiona into your care under my supervision. You could still operate your bakery during the day. What do you say?"

Maggie's tongue felt stuck to the roof of her mouth. If she weren't slipping away with Fiona, she would take Abigail's offer. But she had other plans. More immediate plans to get back her sister. But she couldn't let Abigail know that for that would be the same as telling Sheriff Masters.

As if the thought had brought him through the crowd, the sheriff appeared with glasses of punch. "Here you go, Ma." He gave his mother a glass first, then handed one to Maggie. "I hope you haven't been too hard on Miss O'Keefe."

"Posh! You must call her Maggie, Simon. And Maggie, this is Simon. You'll be seeing way too much of one another to stick to formalities."

Simon's face brightened. "Have you accepted Ma's offer then? She's pretty persuasive when she wants to be."

"Well, what do you say, Maggie?" Abigail stared at her with a challenge in her dark eyes.

"I–I'll think about it," Maggie said desperately. " 'Tis confusing to think in such commotion."

"Very well," Abigail said. "Come to dinner tomorrow at six, and we'll discuss it further. Ah, there you are, Leora. I was beginning to wonder what kept you."

Maggie jerked and turned her head. Leora was alone, and her heart sank. "Where's me sister?" she asked. She stared anxiously behind Leora. Was Fiona still sick? Her heart sank at the thought. She had a lot to answer for. She *had* been negligent.

"Her cold seemed to be returning. I left her home with my sister-in-law," Leora said. Her defiant gaze seemed to dare Maggie to question her answer.

Maggie pressed her lips together. Leora may have won this battle, but the war was far from over. Maggie's thoughts raced over possible options. There had to be a way to get Fiona away from Leora. Maggie would win. She had to.

five

Simon watched the sparkle fade from Maggie's expressive eyes. He'd never seen such beautiful eyes. Like emerald pools they were. He stifled a grimace. He must be daft; that had seemed almost poetic. But something was different about her. He didn't know what it was.

He must seem like a dolt to stare at her the way he did. She was glaring at his sister as though she'd like to grab her and throttle her. And Simon couldn't say as he blamed Maggie. He had his doubts whether the child had been ill enough to keep her home. Even as a child, Leora had been fiercely possessive. He was going to have to stay on top of the situation, or Maggie would be hard-pressed to get her sister back.

As he watched, Maggie's green eyes narrowed, and she stepped closer to Leora. "But sure, and somehow I don't believe you. Fiona was not looking so peaked this afternoon. I think you aim to keep her, but I'm giving you fair warning that you'll not succeed. She is me own flesh and blood, and I know she wants to be with me."

Maggie spun on her heel and stalked off before Leora could answer, but Leora's face reddened, and her lips compressed in a firm line. He'd seldom seen her this riled. Not since they were children. She must want Fiona very badly. Simon didn't understand. She could have her pick of any of the orphanage children. Why had she focused so totally on Fiona? It made no sense to him.

Leora turned her angry face to her brother. "Why did you let her speak to me that way?" she demanded. "I'm your own sister. And what about that child? I wish you'd seen the condition she was in when we found her. You stood up for her in court today. You should be ashamed of yourself."

"I had to say what I believed," Simon said through tight lips. He hung onto his temper by the narrowest margin. "You've become judge and jury to feed your own desires. You haven't honestly evaluated whether Fiona would be better off with her own sister. Have you even thought of anything but what you want? And what does Everett say? Is he as determined as you to steal that child?"

Leora's face reddened even more, and she clenched her fists at her side. "You never take my side," she said bitterly. "But, no, you're the great town sheriff. You think you're always right."

Their mother put up her hand. "That's enough. This is no place to discuss the matter. Why don't you both come to dinner tomorrow? Maggie is coming to discuss helping out at the orphanage in the evenings. Bring the child, Leora. You will make her sick to keep her from the only mother she knows."

Leora's eyes flashed, but she shrugged. "Very well. But you'll both see how much better off she is with me." She turned and walked away, the outline of her back as stiff and unyielding as her attitude.

Simon's mother sighed. "I don't understand where she

gets that harsh spirit. She was such a sweet child."

Simon refused to answer. Leora couldn't get what she wanted from God—a child of her own—so she would force circumstances to fit the next best thing. He sighed. Maybe he was being too hard on Leora. In spite of his words, he had to believe she truly cared about what was best for Fiona. It was too bad she and Maggie couldn't see eye-to-eye.

He mingled with the church folks and tried to keep an eye out for Maggie. He saw no sign of her and wondered if she'd left. He wouldn't blame her if she had. Leora's demeanor would be hard for an independent, outspoken young woman like Maggie to take.

What was it about her that appealed so much to him? He frowned. She was lovely with that stubborn chin and those eyes. Her hair refused to be corralled by pins, escaping in tiny red ringlets around her face. Her beauty was of the unconventional type, not the hothouse, perfectly-turned-out variety he was used to. But somehow he didn't think it had anything to do with her appearance. A zest for life shone out of her face, a suppressed energy in her body that spoke of adventure and a desire to face the world head-on. Whatever it was, Simon wanted to know her better. And if he found she deserved to keep her sister, he'd do all in his power to bring Fiona home to Maggie.

&

Maggie felt as though steam must be escaping from her ears. She had never been so angry in her life. She left the social and made her way back to her house, where she quickly finished packing. She refused to allow that woman to thwart her plans. The last canal boat left at midnight. She could get out to the Bickwell farm, snatch Fiona, and make it back in time to catch the boat. Her heart beat fast at the thought. What if she was discovered? Would she be thrown in jail?

But she wouldn't be found. This was too important. Right and justice were on her side. She would do whatever she had to do to protect Fiona. She pushed away the voice of caution that questioned the wisdom of stealing a child in the middle of the night and hurried toward the livery.

Twilight was approaching, but Maggie wasn't afraid of the dark. She'd run once in the dark, and she could do it again. Love was a higher law than any court in the land. How could she allow Fiona to spend one more night under that shrew's roof? She hurried up Wabash Street and stopped at the livery. She rented a buggy and was soon on her way out of town. As the buggy clattered along the corduroy road, she found her thoughts wandering to Sheriff Masters. Simon. She liked his name. It seemed strong and dependable. She wished she could have known him better. He would have made a stalwart friend, and she could use one.

Maggie was so tired of running, of never settling in one place. She had thought Wabash might be different, that she might find a lasting home here. But she had no home, and she was beginning to think she never would. For a moment doubts assailed her. Was it right to drag Fiona from a stable home? Maybe Leora was right, and Fiona would be better off with a mother and a father in a home she could depend on. But she pushed the doubt away. She couldn't let herself question what had to be done. Not now.

She shivered. Tears pricked her eyes. The thought of never tucking Fiona into bed at night, of never braiding her hair and listening to her singsong voice recite nursery rhymes brought crushing pain. The lights of the Bickwell farm came into view, and the horse quickened his pace. Maggie pushed the doubts away and stopped the buggy under a large maple tree in a clearing near the corral. She tethered the horse and crept toward the house.

Staying in the shadows, she scurried along the edge of the yard, thankful the darkness hid her from view. How could she know where Fiona was? She could be in any of the rooms. Her hands grew clammy with dread. She had to find her sister. Her throat was tight, and she stumbled over a tree root. Her arms pinwheeled to try to maintain her balance; then, with a faint cry, she pitched to the ground. Out of breath, she sat up and listened. Maybe her outcry had been soft enough that no one was alerted.

There was only silence in the house. Breathing a sigh of relief, she stood and tested her aching ankle. Just a mild sprain. Limping slightly, she crept to the nearest window and peered in. She saw a young woman sitting in a rocker, reading a book to a child on the couch. Looking closer, Maggie's heart lurched. Then she saw the child was not Fiona. It was a boy of about ten.

The young woman read aloud. "Let not your heart be troubled: ye believe in God, believe also in me. In my Father's house are many mansions: if it were not so, I would have told you. I go to prepare a place for you. And if I go to prepare a place for you, I will come again, and receive you unto myself; that where I am, there ye may be also."

Something tugged at Maggie's heart. It sounded so peaceful. A mansion in God's house. She'd never heard that verse before, for surely it was the Bible she read from. She had received very little spiritual training. Her fa had not believed in religion and had told her it was a crutch, a weak man's excuse when things didn't turn out as he expected.

For the first time Maggie wondered about God. Did He see her at all? Did He care about her or Fiona? She wished she could believe it was so. Sighing, she crept past the window and peered in the next window. Moonlight streamed in the window and fell on the face of a sleeping child. Fiona! Joy surged in Maggie's heart, and she clutched the windowsill with fingers desperate to stroke Fiona's hair, to touch her soft cheeks.

How could she get her? She would need to stand on something to climb in the window. Maggie crept again to the back of the house and found a woodpile. Most of the wood was already split, but she found a small pile of unsplit logs near the back of the yard. Selecting the largest log she could carry, she lugged it across the yard and placed it under the window.

Standing on it, she eased the window open. Glancing around to make sure no one was about, she stuck her head in the window and worked her body through as quietly as she could. When she was finally in a heap on the floor, she crawled to the door and listened. There was no sound from the other room. She thrust her head through the doorway and looked down the hall. No one was in sight, though she could still hear the murmured drone as the woman read the Bible aloud.

Heartened, Maggie rose to her feet and shut the door. Tiptoeing to the bed, she shook Fiona gently. Fiona muttered, and Maggie clapped her hand gently over her mouth. "Shush, Darlin'—it's me."

Fiona's eyelids flew open, but her cry was muffled by Maggie's hand. "We must get away, Fiona," Maggie whispered. "Can you be very quiet like a mouse?"

Fiona nodded, and Maggie removed her hand. "It's quickly we must move, or they will keep us apart. Let's get you dressed." Moving with the precision of long practice, she dressed Fiona and pulled her shoes and socks on. "You're being so good," Maggie told her softly. "Very quiet. Fa would be proud. Let's go." She took her sister's hand, then hoisted her to the window and let her down. Leaning out the window, she held Fiona's hand until she saw her sister's small feet touch the top of the log.

Fiona held onto the side of the house as she clambered to the ground. "Hurry, Maggie," she said.

Maggie pulled a chest to the window and stood on it, then sat on the windowsill. She slipped out with her feet reaching for contact with the log. When her foot touched the log, she let go of the window. The log tilted, and she landed on the hard ground. Her breath left her, and she lay gasping for air.

Fiona uttered a little squeak and knelt beside her. Her small hands patted Maggie's face. "Does it hurt, Maggie?"

"No." Maggie wheezed and sat up. "I'm fine. Now let's get out of here." She scrambled to her feet and took Fiona's hand. Running through the dead leaves left from last autumn, she thought they would never reach the relative safety of the buggy. But they finally broke through into the clearing. She lifted Fiona to the seat, then climbed up beside her. Touching the whip to the back of the horse, they were off.

Clattering along the road, she kept turning around and looking for someone to follow them. But the road was empty. Maggie wished she knew how to pray. She would ask God to help them escape detection. They passed several other buggies going in the opposite direction, and each time she had Fiona crouch on the floor. It would be just their misfortune to meet up with Leora and Everett Bickwell.

It was nearly eight-thirty by the time Maggie stopped at the house. She managed to load their two small trunks in the buggy. She took off her bonnet and picked up the scissors she'd laid out. Her heart sank at what she was about to do. Her mother had always told her that her hair was her one beauty. But it couldn't be helped. She took a deep breath, then began to hack at the thick locks. Within minutes her hair lay in a heap around her. Her neck felt cold and bare. She was afraid to look in the mirror. For a moment she wondered what Simon would say if he could see her like this. But he would never see her with her hair shorn. In fact, he would never see her again. Strangely, the thought left her feeling sad.

"You look funny, Maggie," Fiona said.

"Now it's your turn," Maggie said, turning to her sister. "We'll be two brothers traveling together." Fiona's eyes grew wide, but she didn't object and held perfectly still as Maggie cut the wispy curls close to her head. "Now let's get dressed. Fa's things fit me fairly well, and you can wear the trousers you play in." She dressed Fiona, then swept the hair into a pile before she picked it up and put it into the stove. She didn't take time to burn it. It was enough that it was hidden.

After they were dressed, she lifted Fiona into the buggy. "Remember—your name is Sean," she told her. "And I'm Duffy."

Fiona nodded, a smile lighting her face. "Just like Fa," she said. Their father, Sean O'Keefe, had carried the name proudly. It was fitting that Fiona wear it during this time of danger.

They went to the canal station. Two burly men took charge of the trunks. She found a spot on the canal boat near some other women. One of them, an older woman with a kind face, agreed to keep an eye on Fiona while Maggie took the buggy back to the livery. She was gone only fifteen minutes. When she returned, Fiona was asleep with her head on the woman's lap.

Maggie sat on the floor beside them and pulled a blanket from her trunk. She moved Fiona onto her lap and covered them both with the blanket. She longed for sleep, for the oblivion it would bring, but rest eluded her. What would Simon do when he found her gone? Would he pursue her or shrug and go on to more pressing business? If his sister had any say in it, she would have her brother combing the area for Maggie and Fiona.

The murky water lapped against the side of the canal boat. Its soothing sound should have lulled her to sleep, but Maggie's eyes remained wide open. Fiona slept soundly, her mouth open and her breathing deep and regular. Maggie leaned her head against the side of the boat. Would the boat never leave? They had to get out of here before they were discovered.

Since they hadn't passed the Bickwells on the way home, it would be at least an hour before any alarm could be raised. Hope tightened her chest. Maybe they would get away. How far should they travel by canal boat? Maybe they should get off at the next stop and take a train. They had to evade the law.

She finally heard the call for departure at midnight. The boat began moving out into the middle of the canal. The horses pulled, their hooves clopping against the rocky soil of the trail. The movement sent a thrill of hope through Maggie. Now maybe she could sleep. She closed her eyes, and her thoughts drifted back to Ireland. Would things have been better if they'd stayed? There was no work for Fa, but maybe things were better now. She wished she could find a safe haven somewhere. But where?

She felt like a vagabond, always traveling and never resting. Would it be this way the remainder of her life? The thought filled her with despair. She had to find somewhere for her and Fiona. There could be no more of this running, no more of this fear and trembling as she waited to be caught. Once her hair grew back and they took back their true identities, she would have Fiona call her "Mum." She should have done it long ago. This wouldn't have happened if Simon hadn't discovered Fiona wasn't her own child.

The boat moved slowly through the night, stopping several times along the canal to load or unload cargo. Maggie couldn't sleep. Every time she started to drift off, someone would snore or another would wake up and shuffle along the deck. When dawn tinged the sky with pink, she nearly groaned aloud. But at least they were away from Wabash. And safe.

six

Simon sighed. This was the first social he'd ever been to where it dragged like a plow in the field. He was aware all evening of Leora's high-pitched laughter. It had a quality of desperation to it, and he had to wonder why keeping Fiona was so important to her. Something in that little girl had touched a chord with her. It was a triangle he didn't know how to fix. And that bothered him. As the eldest, he was the one who drew the brunt of their father's drunken rages. He was used to taking care of Leora, but this was one time when he was helpless.

The festivities broke up around nine. Simon helped clean up and put the chairs away. When the door was shut for the night, he strolled down Miami Street in the moonlight and paused at Maggie's house. No light shone from the windows. Simon felt a stab of disappointment, and he gave a rueful smile. What difference would it make anyway? He couldn't drop by this late. It wouldn't be proper.

He wandered down Canal Street, then went to his office. His rooms were above the office, but he didn't feel like going to bed. He didn't know what he felt like doing, but sleep didn't sound appealing. He dropped into the old chair at his desk and put his boots up on the desk, its top scarred and battered by other boots and spurs.

Bonnie, the deputy's wife, must have cleaned tonight. The floor was swept, and a faint odor of lemon polish hung in the air. The sparkle wouldn't last long, though. With the constant traffic, his office stayed clean for a day out of the week. He sighed and leaned his head against the back of the chair.

How could he help heal this situation between Maggie and Leora? It was ironic. He was the sheriff, the one appointed to defend law and order, with force if necessary; yet he had always been the peacemaker in the family. He hated conflict though he didn't fear it. But he was happiest when everyone got along and peace ruled. He sighed again. Prayer was all that would work. God would have to handle it.

He must have dozed, for a sudden bang woke him, and he jumped, nearly toppling the chair and himself onto the floor. Blinking, he stared at the door. His brother-in-law stood in the doorway, his dark eyes solemn. Everett rarely laughed out loud. He was a sober man, though good and kind to Leora. He was hard to read, though, and Simon had to wonder what his brother-in-law thought of the fight for the child.

"Everett, I thought you'd gone home." Simon planted his feet back on the floor and swiped a hand through his hair.

"Leora sent me. The child is missing." Everett's eyes were wide, and he twisted his hat in his hand. Simon had never seen him so rattled. He must have taken to Fiona as well.

Simon sucked in his breath. "She must have wandered away."

Everett shook his head. "The bedroom window was up and a log dragged under the window. She was taken.

It's my fault. Leora didn't want to leave her tonight, and I insisted."

Maggie. Simon knew it in his bones. With a sinking heart, he remembered the determination on her face when she walked away from his sister's attack. She must have been planning to snatch her sister even then. A lot of good his warning had done. His mouth grim, he stood and grabbed his hat.

"We'd better go see Maggie." He hated to do it, but it was part of his job. Maggie would have to learn that in America the law ruled or there would be anarchy.

Everett held open the door, then followed Simon outside into the crisp March air. The temperature had dropped to close to freezing in the night, and Simon shivered. He hoped Maggie and Fiona weren't out in the elements. Spring weather was so fickle in Indiana. Last year a blizzard had swept through the state, and Simon still remembered how the drifts touched the eaves of his mother's house.

He marched down Canal Street and turned onto Miami. A few minutes later he bounded up the steps to Maggie's porch. He rapped on the door. The wind blew across the porch, and he huddled deeper into his jacket. There was no sound on the other side of the door. He pounded on the door again. "Maggie! I know you've got Fiona. Open the door so we can talk about it." His anger at her disregard for the law mounted with every moment. She wouldn't be there. He knew it in his gut. He'd seen her packing with his own eyes. His own pride had blinded him. He'd thought she would listen to the great Sheriff Masters. How foolish he was! Maybe she was not the woman he thought she was. Maybe his sister was right.

When only silence answered his call, he gripped the doorknob and twisted. It was unlocked. Pushing in to the display room that held the faint scent of baked bread and cookies, he felt for the lamp on the table near the door. His hand touched the matchbox, and he lit the lamp. Holding it high, he stepped farther into the house. "Maggie? Where are you?"

"I don't think anyone is here," Everett said.

The house felt empty. Simon knew they were gone, but he had to make sure. He and Everett walked through the quiet rooms downstairs, then mounted the steps to the upstairs apartment. It was cold up here. Simon shivered. The stove was stone cold. Maggie must have been gone for hours. The rooms were neat and clean, nearly swept clean of belongings. Even the beds were bare of bedding. She must have packed it all and taken it with her. That probably meant she was traveling by train.

Simon wheeled and strode to the steps. "We'd better check the train station. They might still be there." Everett followed him silently.

The wind whistled through the eaves as they exited onto the porch. "What about the canal boat?" Everett asked.

Simon shook his head. "Too slow. She would want to put as many miles as possible between Wabash and Fiona. My bet is on the train. I hope the station master remembers them."

Two men dressed in rough clothing dozed on a bench inside the station. Simon stepped past them and went to the counter.

Harry Wilson, a stocky man of about fifty chewed on his unlit cigar. His rheumy blue eyes were alight with curiosity when he saw Simon. "What brings you out so late, Sheriff?"

Simon pushed his hat back on his head. "We're looking for two sisters, Harry. Maggie and Fiona O'Keefe, though they could be using false names. The older one is seventeen, about five-foot-five with curly red hair and green eyes. Her sister is a miniature of Maggie. You see them?"

Harry chewed deliberately on his cigar, then shook his head. "Nope. I'd remember a couple like that. Mostly single men and a couple of families traveling today. What time would this have been?"

"After eight."

Harry spit the end of his cigar on the floor. "Sorry, Sheriff. They didn't leave by train. What they in trouble for, bank robbery?" He guffawed, his eyes gleaming at his own wit.

Simon didn't smile. Frustration welled inside of him like the spring water outside town. "If you happen to see them, let me know," he said shortly. He wasn't about to satisfy Harry's curiosity at the expense of Maggie's reputation. Didn't she see that running made things worse? His mother was more than willing to help, and he was, too. She'd done a very foolish thing.

He walked away without another word. Everett followed him outside onto the boardwalk. "What now?" Everett asked.

"I'll check at the livery. Maybe she rented a buggy and went to Marion or Lagro to throw us off the trail."

"I think we won't find her," Everett said. "I told Leora

not to get attached to the child. She doesn't belong to us." He cleared his throat. "Though I must admit, the child already has us both wrapped around her little finger. She's quite engaging."

"Leora didn't listen, did she?"

Everett shook his head. "You know your sister well. This obsession for a child drives her." He sighed. "I tell her we must be patient and wait on God, but patience is a virtue she has never had much skill in finding. And my own has gone pretty dry as well."

"She doesn't have much patience." Simon clamped his lips shut. He wouldn't want to do anything to undermine his sister's marriage.

As though he sensed his thoughts, Everett touched Simon's arm. "I love Leora in spite of her faults," he said softly. "She's a good woman, but she carries her torment like an Indian warrior carries his coup. Just pray for her, Simon. She's been happier these past few days than I've seen her in years."

Simon felt shame. What did he know of the torment of childlessness? "You're a wise man, Everett. Leora is lucky to have you."

Everett smiled then. "I am the lucky one," he said. "Leora is strong. And we will weather this storm. I have to say that I pray we are allowed to keep the child, though. She has brought joy to our house."

Simon nodded. But their joy meant Maggie's grief. And he found that the thought bothered him very much. He turned and led the way to the livery. The stable was dark as was the owner's house next door.

"No sense in waking my deputy tonight," he told

Everett. "We might as well wait until daylight to search. We could drive right by them in the dark and never see them."

Everett nodded. "I'd better get home. Leora will be frantic."

"I'm surprised she let you come by yourself," Simon said with a chuckle.

"I didn't give her a choice," Everett said.

The iron in Everett's words surprised Simon. His brother-in-law must possess more backbone than he'd realized. Leora likely knew how far she could push him. He waved good-bye to Everett, then went down the street to his office. Sleep would be hard coming tonight. As he climbed the steps to his apartment over the jail, he prayed for God to keep Maggie safe.

♨

The canal boat moved through the turgid water. Maggie's shorn head felt strange, and the male clothing felt even stranger. Fiona slept until nearly dawn, and Maggie sat stroking her sister's head. When she awoke, Fiona seemed listless and pale. Her short hair made her green eyes, so like Maggie's own, look enormous in her pinched face.

Uneasiness stirred in Maggie's stomach. Had she done the right thing by bringing Fiona out in the elements when she was recovering from a cold? Maggie touched her sister's forehead, but it was cool and dry, and she breathed a sigh of relief.

She grabbed a knapsack and rummaged through it. "You hungry, me darlin'? I brought some muffins for breakfast."

Fiona's face lit up. "With raisins?"

"Lots of raisins." Maggie handed a muffin to Fiona and bit into one herself. She was starved. At the church social she had left before she'd had a chance to eat anything. At the thought of the social, her stomach fluttered again. Surely by now Simon knew she was gone and had taken Fiona with her. Leora would have reported Fiona missing as soon as she returned home. Was he even now looking for her?

She swallowed the muffin dryly. They had to find a place to hide from searchers. But where? She looked over at the woman beside her. "Where are we now?" she asked.

The woman, the same one who had kept an eye on Fiona, had rough, reddened hands that spoke of hard labor, but her face was kind. "My man said we passed Peru in the night and should be coming up on Logansport soon. Where you heading, Lad?"

Maggie's heart lightened. They were leaving Wabash far behind, and her disguise had held so far. "I'm not sure yet," she said. "I need to find work for me and a place for me and me brother."

The woman nodded. "The name's Maisie. Maisie Nelson. My man is Robert. We're moving to Kentucky to live near my parents. My pa is getting up in years and needs help with the farm. What can you do?"

"I–I can cook." As soon as the words were out of her mouth, Maggie knew how ridiculous it sounded. A young man should be talking about blacksmithing or farming, not cooking. The woman's face didn't change, though. She merely nodded and went back to knitting the stockings she was working on.

What *would* she do? She had saved enough money to last for a few weeks, but it was her nest egg to open another bakery. She could say her father had been a baker and had taught her all she knew. Maybe no one would question it. Or she could keep moving until her hair grew out enough to allay suspicion when she took to wearing a dress again.

Her thoughts drifted to Simon again. Was he angry when he found her gone? And why should she care what he thought anyway? He was nothing to her, simply a man who had stuck his nose in her business. The more miles she put between her and the sheriff, the better.

"What did you do at Mrs. Bickwell's house?" Maggie asked Fiona.

Fiona took a sip of the water Maggie offered her, then wiped her mouth with the back of her hand. "She curled my hair, and we played with dollies. She had one with long yellow hair. I liked her. And she sang to me and read me stories."

Maggie felt a pang of remorse. Leora had been kinder than she'd thought. Was she truly upset to discover Fiona gone? *It was for the best,* Maggie told herself. Better to get Fiona away before they both became too attached. Unless it was already too late.

"Did you like it there?" she asked Fiona.

The little girl tilted her head to one side. "Sometimes. But I missed you. Mrs. Bickwell didn't have a little boy or girl. It made her sad. She told me I could be her little girl."

"What did you tell her?" Maggie held her breath.

"I told her I could stay only if you stayed, too." Fiona curled up against Maggie's side and pulled the blanket up under her chin. "I want to be with you. But I wish we could both stay with Mama Leora."

Mama Leora. Maggie struggled to hold her anger in check. How dare she call herself that to Fiona! Clenching her hands into fists at her side, Maggie blinked back tears. She'd done the right thing. Fiona belonged with her, and no one could keep them apart. She glanced over the side of the boat. They were nearing a town. It must be Logansport. It wasn't far enough away from Wabash so Maggie had no interest in looking at it.

She burrowed under the blanket again until the sun could warm up the air. What would this day and the day after hold? The thought of the future loomed like an impenetrable forest, and she wasn't strong enough to face it yet. Weariness slowed her thoughts and sapped her courage. The struggle seemed never ending. Would she ever be free? Was there a home for her someday, a place she would feel safe? It didn't seem likely to Maggie as she finally closed her eyes and slept.

seven

Simon fumed as he stepped back onto the boardwalk and strode toward his office. No one seemed to have seen them, and he had no idea where to look next. As near as he could tell, she had no friends who would have hidden her, nor could he believe that anyone had lied to cover her escape. The people he had questioned at the train station and at the canal lock had been very adamant about not seeing a woman and little girl traveling alone. With Maggie's beautiful hair, it wasn't likely she could be missed, even without the little girl.

He didn't want to examine why he was so determined to find her. If she was gone from Wabash, he could easily let the responsibility slide to some other sheriff in some other town.

But for some reason he couldn't do that. There was something about Maggie that drew him. Maybe it was that little-girl-lost look that hovered around her eyes when she thought no one was looking. As long as she was running, she would never lose the fear that lurked there. *It was time to end it,* he told himself.

Simon cut across in front of a wagon laden with sacks of feed and hurried down Miami Street toward Maggie's house. He would check out her house one more time in the daylight. Maybe he'd missed some clue to her intentions. Maggie was so young, too young to be so devious that he couldn't find her.

He pushed open the door and entered the pastry display room. It already had an abandoned feel to it. He went through the door to the kitchen and poked around in the cupboards and the pantry. Nothing. Discouraged, he climbed the back stairway to the living quarters. Searching the closets, all he found was dust and a pair of battered shoes with holes in the soles. Nothing that gave him any idea of where to look next.

Simon went back downstairs and gazed around the display room one last time. She had covered her tracks well. Too well. The display room had been swept clean. He picked up the broom lying in his path and thumped it on the floor in frustration. A curl of red hair skittered across the floor from the force of his thump, evidently dislodged from the broom.

Simon knelt and picked it up. He stared at it for a moment, then looked at the stove thoughtfully. Stepping to the stove, he stooped and flipped open the door. A mass of red hair on the cold embers. He took out a handful and rubbed its luxurious softness between his fingers. Maggie's hair. And maybe Fiona's as well.

His heart clenched. Her beautiful hair, all shorn and discarded like so much refuse. How could she do it? It showed the depth of her determination to keep Fiona with her. Simon wished she hadn't done it; then he mentally shook himself. What business was it of his if she wanted to shave her head bald? But the regret wouldn't go away.

His mouth in a grim line, he scooped up the hair and stuffed it in his bandana, then shut the stove and stood. His thoughts shied away from why he was keeping her hair. It was evidence, nothing more. She was disguised as a young man, and likely Fiona was dressed as a boy. That would change things considerably. Simon's heart lightened. They couldn't have gone far. He hurried toward the train station. Two brothers had been traveling to Cincinnati yesterday, but when he checked the register, he saw it was a family he knew here in town. The Daggerts traveled to Ohio several times a year to visit family.

He thanked the clerk, then went down to check the canal boat schedule. He probably should have done it last night. The clerk, a sleepy-eyed young man, twitched his thin mustache and told him two brothers had been traveling last night by boat as well. A Duffy Ogan and his younger brother Sean. Simon grinned. It had to be Maggie and Fiona.

"Where does the boat stop?"

"Ten places between here and Evansville," the man told him.

Simon's smile faded, and he nearly groaned. With the head start she had, she could be anywhere. For a moment he was tempted to give up; then he set his jaw. She had to learn she couldn't flaunt the law this way. And Fiona had been in no shape to travel. It showed very poor judgment on Maggie's part to take the child out into the chilly night air when she was recovering from a bad cold. He had his duty, and he would carry it out.

❧

The muddy canal water added to the unkempt way Maggie felt. She rubbed her burning eyes and turned around to stare forward. She wished she and Fiona could get off here and try to find lodging. The thought of a soft bed was like a glimpse of heaven.

Maggie pushed the thought away. Heaven seemed far away and unreal. It was a place she'd never see, especially now that she had to add being a criminal on the run to her other sins. Logansport wasn't nearly far enough from danger. Fiona's small hand crept into hers.

"Are we almost there?" Fiona's voice was faint and tired.

Maggie looked down and frowned. Fiona's cheeks were flushed and her eyes overly bright. She felt her sister's forehead and nearly snatched her hand away at the burning heat radiating from the small face. "But sure, and you're as hot as a brick on a sunny day."

"I don't feel so good," Fiona said. "Can I sleep now?" Her words were a little slurred, and Maggie gathered her up in alarm.

"Rest, little one," she whispered as Fiona laid her head on Maggie's shoulder. She had to get Fiona off this boat and in a quiet place. Maybe with some rest she would be better tomorrow. Maggie clung to that hope. For it was clear, even if she could afford a doctor, it would be dangerous to take Fiona to one. Not only would their covers be blown, but that meddling sheriff would be there within hours. He was likely on their trail even now.

She laid Fiona on a pallet on the deck, then dipped a corner of her shirt in the barrel of water on the deck and sponged Fiona's face. The little girl sighed in her sleep at the cool relief. Maggie stayed at her side until she heard the boat go through the lock at Logansport. Then she gently shook Fiona awake.

"Come along, me darlin'," she whispered. She hired a

young lad to take charge of their trunk while she carried Fiona. She hated to spend the money, paltry a charge as it was, but she had no choice. She needed to find a place for Fiona as quickly as possible.

An older woman on the boardwalk outside the general store directed her to a boardinghouse at the end of the block. The proprietor told her a room was still available, though he stared suspiciously at the sick child in Maggie's arms.

"That kid ain't got nothing bad like cholera, does he?" he asked gruffly.

Maggie shook her head. "Me brother is just recovering from a cold," she said. She wished she could claim Fiona to be her son, but she knew that masquerading as a boy she looked even younger than her seventeen years. She didn't dare arouse any more suspicions.

She and her hired boy followed the proprietor up narrow stairs to a room at the end of the hall. It was small but clean. The furnishings were meager, but they would do. At least it was a roof over their heads, a place for Fiona to recover. Then they would push on, farther away from Wabash and its meddling sheriff.

"There's water in the pitcher on the dresser," the proprietor said.

Thanking him, she waited until he pulled the door shut behind him and the boy. Then she laid Fiona on the bed, pulled off the child's boots, and quickly undressed her. She poured water from the pitcher into the bowl, opened the trunk, and tore a length of cloth from one of her petticoats. Dipping it in the cool water, she began to sponge Fiona.

Her sister shivered and complained, but Maggie continued until Fiona's body began to cool. Then she covered her with a sheet and let her sleep. Maggie wanted nothing more than to crawl into the bed with her sister and pull the covers over her head, but she didn't dare. There was too much to do. She had to find work. Her bit of money wouldn't hold out for long, especially if Fiona was really sick. Money would have to be spent for a doctor as well, if Fiona wasn't better by morning. Maggie clung to that hope. Fiona *had* to be well.

She knelt and shook Fiona gently. "I must go out for a bit, Dearie. Don't leave the room—just rest."

Fiona opened her eyes and stared at Maggie with bewildered eyes. "I want to go with you," she said plaintively.

"But sure, and you're sick, me girl. I won't be gone but two ticks. You sleep, and I'll bring you back something to eat."

Fiona nodded, but tears pooled in her eyes. Then her eyes closed, and her long lashes lay against the curve of her cheeks. Love welled up in Maggie's heart, and she kissed Fiona's forehead. "Sleep well, me girl."

She stood with purpose. What kind of work could she do as a man? It must be something that wasn't physically tougher than she could manage, and it had to be someplace where she could escape detection as to her true gender. Maggie crammed her hat onto her head and went out.

The proprietor was not at his desk, and Maggie was thankful for that. She wasn't up to more questions. She stepped out into the sunshine and walked down the street. A mercantile on the corner had a sign in the window. WANTED: DELIVERY BOY. She stopped in the street and was nearly run down by a burly man in a suit who wasn't prepared for her to halt abruptly in the walkway.

"Watch what you're doing, Kid," he growled as he brushed by her.

Maggie didn't respond; she just stared at the sign. *Delivery boy.* She could do that. Her heart began to thump against her ribs. It surely couldn't be that easy, could it? Her hand shook a little as she pushed open the screen door and stepped inside.

An older woman with round cheeks and soft gray eyes looked up from behind the counter. "May I help you?" she asked.

"The—the sign in the window," Maggie stammered. "It said you're looking for a delivery boy?"

The woman appraised her, and her forehead wrinkled. "You're not very big," she said. "Some of the bags and barrels can get mighty heavy."

"I'm stronger than I look," Maggie said hastily. But was she strong enough? "But sure, and you'll find me a hard worker. I stick to a job until it's done."

The woman's frown didn't fade, and Maggie thought she saw a refusal forming on the woman's lips. "Please, Ma'am, I'm desperate. Me brother is sick, and I need to make some money to take care of him."

The woman's face softened, and she sighed. "What's your name, Lad? You have the look of the Irish about you and in your speech."

"It's Duffy, Ma'am. Duffy Ogan. And sure, but you've got a good ear. Me family came over from the Old Country five years ago." Her heart sped up with hope.

"Very well, Duffy. I'm a sucker for a hard luck story.

We'll give you a try."

A smile lifted the corners of Maggie's mouth, and she felt almost lightheaded with relief. "When do you want me to start, Ma'am?"

"This afternoon, if possible." She shook her head. "I'll likely regret this," she said as she opened the cash register. She handed Maggie some money. "I'll give you an advance on your wages so you can get the doctor to look at your brother. Dr. Layman's office is next door. Come back when he's checked out your brother. How old is the child?"

"Three, Ma'am." Trying not to cry, Maggie took the money. "I thank you kindly, Ma'am. I'll be back as quick as I can."

"Fine." She gave Maggie a wry grin. "Somehow I think you might show up and not take my money and run."

"Oh, no, Ma'am, I wouldn't do something like that!" Maggie widened her eyes. Did the woman think she was a thief?

"I'm Norma Watson," the woman said. "And for some reason I believe you." She nodded toward the door. "Now get along with you to the doctor's office."

Maggie managed a smile. "Thank you, Mrs. Watson. You won't regret it." She opened the door and practically ran from the shop. There were still good people left in the world. Maybe this town could be a place where she could finally settle. A coldness gripped her. But it was probably too close to Wabash.

She rushed into the doctor's office. A kind-faced older woman promised to send the doctor around right away. Maggie hurried back to the boardinghouse. She'd been gone less than an hour, but she knew it was still too long to leave a child as young as Fiona alone, especially sick. Her mouth dry with dread, she threw open the door and ran up the stairs.

Guilt gnawed at her as she pushed open the door to her room. Was she wrong to take Fiona? With Leora Bickwell she would have her own room and good food. Maggie pushed the traitorous thoughts away. She loved Fiona. No one else could love Fiona as Maggie did.

But what would they do? How could they live? She needed to find someone to care for Fiona while she worked. Leaving her wasn't an option. Relief flooded her when she saw Fiona still sleeping. But when she touched her, the smile faltered. Fiona was so hot. Terror gripped her, and she began to sponge the little girl with cool water again. *Dip, wring, wipe. Dip, wring, wipe.* It seemed she labored for hours over Fiona before the little body began to cool again. Would the doctor never come?

Finally she heard the heavy tread on the steps, then a knock on her door. She rushed to the door and threw it open.

Dr. Layman carried his black bag. His gaze darted past Maggie to the small figure on the bed. He frowned and pushed past Maggie. She followed closely behind. Setting his bag on the bed, he opened it and drew out his stethoscope. He placed it on Fiona's chest and listened.

His frown deepened, and Maggie's breath caught in her throat. "What is it? What's wrong?"

"Pneumonia," Dr. Layman said. "You're going to need to keep a close watch on him." He rummaged in his bag again. "I have some medicine to give him, but I won't lie to you. It will be touch and go. Keep sponging him off. I'll check back on him every hour." He placed a hand on her shoulder. "Good luck."

Good luck? That was the best he could do? Maggie stared at his retreating back in disbelief. Fiona had to be all right! Maggie couldn't bear it if— She broke off the thought, unable to tolerate the alternative. She covered her face with her hands and sobbed. Drawing a shuddering breath, she lifted her head. She suddenly wished the sheriff were here. In spite of his meddling, he brought such a sense of stability, of confidence. She squared her shoulders. But he wasn't here; there was no one for Fiona but her. And she had no time to waste on tears.

She poured more water in the bowl, then went to work. Her hands grew red and chapped from the constant contact with water, and her shoulders ached. She considered it just punishment for snatching Fiona from a safe and comfortable home. Maggie realized she had been foolish, very foolish. And Fiona was paying the price.

The doctor checked back several times through the long day, but each visit his expression grew grimmer. Maggie's hope began to fade, but she pushed on. She wished she had someone she could lean on, some other person who would share her burden. But she and Fiona were all alone. A picture of Simon's strong shoulders and kind eyes flashed through her mind, but she pushed it away. She didn't deserve anyone to help her. She'd caused this herself. Her determination to have her own way had led her and Fiona down this dark path.

Near suppertime she sat on the floor beside the bed and leaned her head against the mattress. Her eyes burned with weariness and unshed tears. Fiona still clung to life, her breathing labored and shallow. Maggie wished she knew how to pray. If Simon were here, he would know how to pray, and God would listen to him.

The murmur of crowds in the street drifted softly through the window. Late afternoon rays of sunlight filtered through the window. The approaching night brought terror. Dread congealed in Maggie's stomach, and she wished she could pull the covers over her head and refuse to face what this night might hold. She stood to her feet and went to the pitcher to pour fresh water.

Footsteps came up the stairs, followed by a knock on the door. Eager to have the doctor's opinion, she hurried to the door and threw it open. Simon Masters stood before her, his broad shoulders spanning the doorway. He looked so solid, so reliable to Maggie that she felt nearly faint with relief. She launched herself against his chest and burst into noisy sobs.

"Me sister, Simon—you were right," she babbled through her tears. "Never should I have taken her from Leora. It's sorry I am."

After a slight hesitation, his arms came around her, and he held her while she sobbed out her fear and despair. She knew when he saw Fiona's small form on the bed, for he stiffened and pulled away. His large hands gripped her shoulders, and he set her gently aside. Striding to the bed, he touched Fiona's head.

Maggie crowded in close behind him. " 'Tis pneumonia, it is," she said softly. "Nothing I do seems to relieve her suffering. But sure, and I was wishing you would come. You can pray for her." For the first time since Mum and Fa had gone, she believed God might still care. For surely hadn't He sent Simon to her? There was no other explanation to Maggie's mind.

She expected to see disgust and disapproval on Simon's face when he turned to look at her, but all she saw was compassion and concern.

"How long has she been like this? Has the doctor been here?" he asked.

Maggie nodded. "Aye. He says it's in God's hands. Would you pray for her?" She held her breath as she waited for his reply.

Simon nodded. He gripped Maggie's hand, and together they knelt beside Fiona's bed. Simon laid his other hand on Fiona's head and began to pray. Maggie's heart calmed within her as he asked God for mercy and for healing. His deep voice filled her with awe as he pleaded with God for Fiona's life. He really cared, and for a few minutes Maggie could believe that God cared as well.

When the prayer ended, she lifted her head to peek at her sister. She saw no perceptible change yet, and her heart fell.

Simon must have seen her disappointment, for he squeezed her hand. "I'll sit with her. You get some rest. She's going to be fine."

Maggie was afraid to hope he knew what he was talking about. But she was so glad to be able to leave Fiona's well-being in his hands. She nodded and crawled onto the other side of the bed. If she knew how to pray, she would thank God for sending Simon no matter what the outcome. But since she didn't, she merely closed her eyes and slept.

eight

Simon struggled to keep his judgments fair, though he wanted to ask Maggie what she had been thinking to take a sick child out in the unpredictable spring weather. Fiona's condition was further evidence of Maggie's immaturity. All she'd thought of was what *she* wanted, not what was best for Fiona. But she was too upset to challenge right now. And to be honest, he didn't want to make her hate him more than she already did.

He glanced at her hair and felt a pang of remorse. All those glorious red curls, hacked off and left lying in the stove like rubbish. It seemed a sacrilege to Simon, but it showed Maggie's desperation. He felt regretful that she had been so afraid she couldn't trust him to work it out for the best. Dressed in tattered pants and a threadbare shirt, she looked like a twelve-year-old boy with a very bad haircut. Her red hair was ragged and uneven, but he had to admit to himself that in his eyes she was still beautiful.

He didn't understand it. Women more beautiful than Maggie had set their caps on him. They had been easy to resist. Maggie made no effort to hide her disdain, and he was drawn to her like a moth to the flame.

He pulled his gaze from her sleeping face and settled down to keep watch through the long night. The hours dragged on. Maggie awakened and stretched as shafts of sunlight made their way through the window. Just after dawn Fiona stirred. Simon watched as Maggie immediately crouched beside the bed.

She touched the child's sweat-soaked hair. "But sure, and you're going to be fine, me girl. Would you like some water?" Her voice was overly loud with relief.

Fiona nodded, and Maggie lifted a cup of water to her sister's lips and held it while Fiona struggled to sip it. Finally Fiona lay back against the pillow, her small face white with exhaustion. Maggie's face didn't look much better. All the condemnation Simon had pent up inside ebbed away. She loved Fiona, and he couldn't fault her for that. But the consequences would still have to be paid. No matter the depth of her love, what she had done was wrong and willful. He swallowed hard as Maggie lavished her love and attention on the sick child. Would anyone ever love him that way?

"Thank you for praying," Maggie whispered when Fiona drifted off to sleep again. "But sure, and I know she would have died but for you."

"But for God," Simon corrected. "I did nothing."

"You prayed. God wouldn't listen to the likes of me." Tears trembled on the edges of her lashes, and the last of Simon's anger evaporated.

He sighed. She needed to understand God's love and mercy, but she had received so little spiritual training that it was hard to know how to reach her. Before he could frame an answer, she stood and walked toward the door.

" 'Tis late to work I'll be if I don't hurry," she told him. "Fiona will sleep, if you want to get some rest yourself."

"We're going back to Wabash. And I'm not letting

you out of my sight."

Her jaw stiffened. "Me sister will need to recover before we can think about going back to Wabash. And I took an advance on me wages at the mercantile. I'll work it off before we leave."

"I'll pay it back. You don't need to worry about it." Even as he offered, he knew she'd never accept it. That stiff-necked Irish pride of hers would insist on paying her own debts.

Maggie shook her head. "No, me boyo, you'll not be paying me bills. 'Tis me own debt, and these two hands will earn me own way."

"You haven't proven yourself trustworthy, Maggie." He stepped toward the door to detain her, but with a flicker of alarm in her eyes, she opened the door and dashed down the steps. He thought of following her, but Fiona could not be left alone. And the doctor was due back at any time. Simon was eager to hear what he had to say. And whatever he thought of Maggie's tendency to run, she wouldn't leave Fiona. That much was certain.

He shut the door and went to the worn armchair in the corner of the room. Sinking into its well-sprung depths, he felt a niggling sense of respect for Maggie. Young and foolish she might be, but she had a strong sense of responsibility. Many women would have taken him up on his no-strings offer to repay a debt. But he was beginning to realize Maggie wasn't like most women. In fact, she was unlike any other woman he'd ever met.

But she was going to hate him when this was all over. She feared and despised him now; once the finality sank in, she would truly hate him. There was no way around that fact. The thought saddened Simon. He leaned his head against the back of the chair and closed his eyes. When he awoke, sunlight was streaming in the window, and someone was pounding on the door. Shaking the sleep from his eyes, he stood and hurried to the door.

The man in the doorway stared at him a moment, then brushed past him. "You the child's father?"

"You must be the doctor. Come in." He stepped aside to allow the doctor to enter, then followed the burly form to Fiona's bedside. "He's better, I think. His breathing eased about dawn."

The doctor put his stethoscope to Fiona's back and listened. The satisfaction on his face gave Simon hope. Fiona awoke and smiled at them both. Her eyes were clear and focused, and Simon wanted to shout with relief.

The doctor nodded. "The crisis has passed. I thought this little boy was a goner. What did you do for him?"

"Just prayed."

The doctor nodded. "The very best medicine. We seem to have a bona fide miracle here." He put his stethoscope away and closed his bag. "He'll be weak and shaky for a good week. Keep him quiet and see that he gets plenty of water and good food. Call me if you need me."

When the doctor was gone, Simon fixed the child some bread with jam. She stared at him the entire time she ate, her green eyes huge in her pinched face. She obviously thought him an ogre, and he really couldn't blame her. He was the mean bully bent on ripping her away from her beloved sister. And the fact that his own sister was the one determined to keep her didn't help matters any.

"Want more?" he asked.

Fiona tucked her chin against her neck and shook her head. "I want Maggie," she whispered. Tears rolled from her eyes, and her little bow of a mouth trembled.

Simon suppressed a sigh of exasperation. He had no idea of how to deal with a crying child. The only experience he had with children was when they came tearing past him at church. "Why don't you lie back down and go to sleep? Maggie isn't here right now."

More tears trickled from her eyes. She screwed up her face and began to wail. "I want Maggie!"

"Shush, it's all right. Maggie's at work. She'll be back in a little while." He patted her head awkwardly, then frowned. No wonder she didn't respond; he'd patted her as if she were a dog. But how did one go about quieting a sick child? He gazed around the tiny room. No books, no toys scattered about.

"How about I tell you a story?" he asked. He could hear the desperation in his voice, but Fiona didn't seem to notice. Her tears dried, and she stared at him with expectancy in her eyes. Now what? He didn't have the vaguest idea of what kind of story he could tell. Any fairy tales he had heard had been forgotten long ago.

He thrust his hand into his pocket, and his fingers touched his small Bible. Ah, he could tell her a story out of the Bible. David and Goliath. Every child thrilled to the story. He cleared his throat. "Have you ever heard the story about the little boy who killed a giant and saved the nation of Israel?"

Fiona shook her head and plopped her thumb in her mouth. She scooted a fraction of an inch closer to him.

Encouraged, he pulled his chair next to the bed and plunged into the tale. As he told of Goliath and how big and mean and strong he was, Fiona's eyes grew huge. Then he told her about how David had faith that God would save him from the giant, that He would save the nation of Israel from the Philistines.

All pretense of sucking her thumb gone, Fiona's mouth dropped open when he told how David felled the giant with a small stone. How God was strong and powerful to protect the weak and poor. Simon's heart fairly leaped within him when Fiona's small hand crept across the coverlet to touch his fingers.

"Can you tell me another story about God?" she asked.

She was like a thirsty sponge, Simon reflected. He reckoned she'd never heard much about God in her short life. "Mind if I crawl on that bed next to you?" he asked. "I'm mighty tired." He hadn't slept much for two nights.

Fiona nodded and moved over to make room. He lay on top of the covers and put one hand under his head. What could he tell her about next? Daniel in the lion's den. That was a good one, too.

As he told about Daniel's faith and devotion to God in the face of great difficulty, Fiona's head began to nod. It was all Simon could do to make his voice drone on until she finally slept. Then he closed his eyes. He would take just a small nap. Then he'd be ready to deal with Maggie when she returned.

❧

Maggie's back ached, and her hands bled where blisters had formed and broken open. But a sense of satisfaction made the pain worth the effort. She'd explained to her employer what had happened, and Mrs. Watson had been very understanding. She clucked her tongue and gave Maggie some mustard packs that she guaranteed would help. Then she put Maggie to work.

Maggie had hauled barrels of pickles and sacks of potatoes all over town. Another two days and she would have worked off the advance Mrs. Watson had given her. It was a heady thought to know she would be able to leave town with a clear conscience.

Her male clothing felt odd. Maggie tugged at her shirtsleeve and started down the street toward the boardinghouse. The cool air touched her neck, and she shivered. She wished she still had her hair. She'd seen the shock in Simon's eyes when his gaze lingered on her ragged haircut. Mum always said a girl was wise to face things squarely, and Maggie was honest enough to admit to herself she'd seen the admiration in the sheriff's face as they'd searched for Fiona. She was also honest enough to admit it had been unwilling admiration. He may have liked her looks, but he didn't care much for who she was inside.

She wished they could have met under different circumstances. Who knows what might have happened if they'd met at a social? She would have glided into the room in a dress as green as the soft grass in the meadow back in Ireland, a green that deepened the color of her eyes. He would have asked her to dance and brought her punch and cake.

Maggie's lips tightened. What an *eejit* she was! Daydreaming about the man who had followed her out of town only to drag her back to face the law. Well, she didn't care much for his high-handed manner. And he wasn't going to take her sister away from her. She'd fight with every breath left in her body to keep that from happening.

Her steps dragged as she mounted the stairs and reached for the door. Pushing it open quietly so as not to awaken Fiona, she stopped in the doorway with her mouth open. Fiona lay under the coverlet, her small hand clasped in Simon's large one. He lay curled protectively around Fiona on top of the coverlet. They were both asleep. An occasional snore rattled the window.

Maggie's lips twitched. She didn't know whether to laugh at the strange sight or be hurt that Fiona had taken to him so quickly. He was the enemy. She would have thought even Fiona would understand that.

Closing the door softly behind her, she hung her battered cap on a hook on the back of the door, then sank into the armchair. Simon had dragged it to the edge of the bed, and that was fine with Maggie. She wanted to be as close to Fiona as she could. Her gaze traveled over her sister's small face. She looked better. Much better, in fact, than she had when Maggie left this morning. Hope stirred in her heart. She was going to be all right.

Simon uttered another soft snore, and Maggie's gaze shot to his face. She felt a thrill that she could stare at him to her heart's content and he wouldn't know. For such a big man he looked surprisingly gentle and vulnerable right now. Though not classically handsome, with a nose that looked as if it had been broken a time or two and a cleft chin, Simon appealed to her in ways she didn't understand. He was her enemy—why couldn't she seem to remember that?

His hair looked as if it needed a trim, and his hands, wide and capable-looking, held Fiona securely. He looked solid, Maggie decided. Maybe that's what the attraction was. He was the kind of man who would make sure every detail was taken care of for his family. Tears stung Maggie's eyes. Reliable, that was the word she was searching for.

She wished she dared to touch his thick hair, just to see what it felt like. But it would awaken him, and what could she say? It would be humiliating. She sighed. Simon's eyes flew open, and he gazed into Maggie's face.

Unguarded from his sleep, he smiled a slow, lazy grin that set Maggie's heart soaring. He almost looked as though he were glad to see her. The attraction she'd sensed was there in full force. She couldn't seem to quit staring, but neither could he. They were tied like two cats over a clothesline, but neither of them struggled to break free. His stare did funny things to her insides, things she was afraid to name.

He untangled one hand from Fiona, then reached out and touched Maggie's cheek. "Your lovely hair is gone," he said. "But you're still beautiful. I wish you weren't." His voice was full of regret, and his eyes seemed haunted.

"Why?" she whispered. She leaned her cheek against his hand. His fingers were rough and smelled of soap. Maggie wanted the moment to go on forever.

He didn't answer, but a certain awareness crept over his face, a reserve that hadn't been there before. He sat up and pulled his hand away. The action awoke Fiona. She rubbed her eyes, and a smile spread across her face when she saw Maggie.

"The sheriff told me stories, Maggie," she said, "about a little boy named David. God saved him from the giant, and God can save us from enemies, too, even the sheriff. God won't make me leave you, will He?"

Simon's head jerked as though he'd been slapped. His eyes widened, and Maggie felt sorry for the hurt she saw in his face. But what could she say? Fiona was right. They needed saving from the sheriff. But she wasn't holding out much hope for God's intervention. The sheriff was a praying man, and she was only an Irish immigrant with no money and no prospects. Those odds were pretty overwhelming. If God was going to listen to someone, it wouldn't be her. But she couldn't dash the child's hopes.

"But sure, and didn't I tell you we'd be fine?" she asked. "We're going back to Wabash and see our friends there."

"We don't have any friends," Fiona said. Then her face brightened. "I forgot to tell you. I have a kitten. Her name is Riva. Leora said she was all mine."

Leora again. Maggie's heart clenched. "That was kind of Mrs. Bickwell. You mustn't call her Leora, Fiona."

Fiona stuck out her lip. "She told me to."

Simon scooped up the little girl. "You're getting awfully feisty. I'd say you were feeling better. How about I go get some chow at the café down the street? Are you hungry?"

Fiona nodded, and Maggie's stomach growled. Simon grinned. "I'd say you could both use a good feeding. I'll be back in a little while." He narrowed his eyes and stared at Maggie. "Do I have your word you won't try to run again?"

Maggie swallowed and nodded. "But sure, and what

good would it do to leave? You would track me down again."

Simon nodded. "That I would." He deposited Fiona on Maggie's lap and went toward the door.

As soon as the door shut behind him, Maggie let out the breath she'd been holding. She needed to guard her heart. The last thing she needed was to make cow's eyes at the sheriff. And the last woman he would think of loving would be someone like her who was suspected of neglecting a child. He had a position in the community to uphold. She'd best put all thoughts of Sheriff Simon Masters far away.

nine

"Don't you think it's time you told your employer the truth?"

Simon's words smote Maggie's heart. She'd been plagued with guilt every time she went to work these past three days. Simon was chafing to get back to Wabash, but he'd reluctantly taken a room at the boardinghouse and allowed her to work off her debt. The extra time also allowed Fiona to gather her strength back. It was a small victory, but one that allowed Maggie to hold her head up. Except for the lies she was living with her employer.

Maggie dropped her head. " 'Tis true she needs to know," she admitted. "And today is the last day I need to work. But sure, and it won't be pleasant to tell her."

Simon nodded. "Making things right never is. But it's what God expects of us."

Heat flooded Maggie's face. She thought so seldom about what God wanted. She tried *not* to think of Him at all. But Simon made her want to think about Him, to be better than she was. There was no getting around the way he made her heart come up into her throat with admiration for the kind of man he was. Every day she watched him with Fiona and saw his strength tempered with kindness and gentleness. Fiona adored him already. She no longer thought of him as the enemy.

And Maggie guessed she didn't, either. He was too

kind to be an enemy. And though she might not agree with what he was doing to them, she knew he was only doing his job. Maybe Maggie was wrong to try to keep Fiona with her. Simon would be her uncle if Leora kept Fiona. He could provide some much needed stability and love. But every time Maggie thought about allowing things to run their course, a spirit of determination and rebellion hardened in her. She'd fought too long and hard to keep her sister. She couldn't stop now.

"But sure, and you're right," she told him. "I'll tell Mrs. Watson the truth and beg her forgiveness." The thought made her chest pound with anxiety. An apology was never easy, and this one would be particularly difficult after Mrs. Watson had been so good to her.

Clapping her hat on her head, Maggie left Simon in charge of Fiona and made her way down the street to work. Mrs. Watson was sweeping off the front stoop and smiled when she saw Maggie.

"There you are! I have a delivery ready for you on the counter. It goes to Mrs. Miller two blocks over. The address is on the box."

"Could I talk to you first, Ma'am?" Maggie's heart was pounding so hard she found it hard to breathe.

"Well, of course, Lad. What is it?"

The concern in Mrs. Watson's face made Maggie feel worse. She took a deep breath. "But sure, and 'tis ashamed I am to be telling you this. I must ask your pardon for not being honest." She swept her hat from her head. " 'Tis not a boyo I am, but a lass. Me name is Maggie. Maggie O'Keefe. Fiona is me own dear sister, though, and the rest of what I've told you is true. She really was sick, and I had to find a job." She blurted the words out in a rush.

Mrs. Watson frowned and took Maggie by the chin, tipping her face up to the light. "Well, land's sake, Child, so you are! I must be going blind in my old age to have the wool pulled over my eyes that way. But why did you lie about it? You could have found a job as a seamstress or maybe worked behind the counter." She released Maggie's chin. "You mean to tell me you've been hauling heavy boxes around town and you're just a young girl? Where are your parents?"

Maggie dropped her head. "The law was looking for us. They say I'm too young to care for Fiona." She lifted her head and raised her voice. "But sure, and haven't I been looking after us both for three years? They want to take Fiona from me."

Mrs. Watson's face softened. "Well, Maggie, sometimes we don't see the ways of the Lord. I've seen a peck of trouble come when we insist on having our own way. You must pray and trust God for the right." She touched Maggie's shoulder. "You've worked off the money I loaned you. But I can't pay as much for a shop girl. Can you sew?"

Maggie's heart was touched by Mrs. Watson's generosity. "But sure, and that's the rest of the story. The sheriff from Wabash has found me. I must go back there with him. Fiona must go to another family until the judge decides what's to be done."

"I see." Mrs. Watson's face fell, but she patted Maggie's shoulder, then let her hand drop back to her side. "It's for the best, I'm sure, dear girl. You're mighty young to be saddled with the care of a child. How old are you anyway?"

"But sure, and 'tis nearly eighteen I am! And Fiona is no burden at all. We must stay together! I promised me mum."

"You look but about fourteen," Mrs. Watson observed.

" 'Tis from the haircut and the male clothing," Maggie said. "I owned a bakery in Wabash and saw to all our needs. 'Tis only the law that's meddled with our lives."

"Well, that may be, but have you considered that the law might be right? Maybe Fiona needs a mother *and* a father. You'll always be her sister. It's difficult to make a child feel loved without a real family." Mrs. Watson held up her hand when Maggie would have protested. "You pray about it, my girl. Now run along with you. It's been nice knowing you, Maggie O'Keefe. If you're ever in town again, you be sure to stop by and say howdy." Mrs. Watson hugged Maggie, then gave her a gentle shove.

Maggie's feet dragged as she went back to the boardinghouse. Now they would have to return to Wabash. The thought of facing people who knew her made her shudder. They would stare at her shorn hair and talk about her behind her back. She had to admit they had made her feel welcome in the months since she'd arrived, though. But people always talked. A juicy story like hers would be sure to be the topic of dinner tables all over the county.

Through the closed door she could hear Simon telling Fiona yet another Bible story. The man seemed to have an unlimited supply. Maggie pushed open the door and found Fiona on Simon's lap in the rocker by the window. Her sister's cheeks were pink with color, and her eyes sparkled. How could Maggie argue with that kind of miracle? If Simon hadn't found them, hadn't prayed for Fiona, things would probably be very different.

Simon's head jerked up at the sound of the door. "You're back already?" He studied Maggie's face. "You're upset."

"But sure, and don't I have a right to be upset? You're dragging me back to that town where people will stare and laugh." Maggie crossed her arms over her chest and glared at him. " 'Tis easy for you—they're all your friends. And Leora's friends. I have no chance to keep me sister with me." Tears closed her throat.

Simon put Fiona gently on the floor and stood. Crossing the room, he touched Maggie's shoulder. "You're not leaving room for God to work, Maggie. I promised I'd do the best I could to keep the two of you together. Maybe I can talk the judge into letting both of you stay at the orphanage instead of making Fiona go to Leora's."

Hope surged in Maggie's heart. "But sure, and do you think he would allow it?" As long as they could stay together, the rest was only temporary. She would figure out a way to work things out if they were only together.

"We can only try."

Maggie's shoulders drooped. "But 'tis true the judge is related somehow, isn't he? It seemed pretty clear at the trial. He may not be willing to upset her."

"He is Everett's cousin," Simon said with obvious reluctance.

Maggie nodded. She had sensed as much. Her case was hopeless, but she couldn't give up the fight.

Simon rushed on as though he sensed her despair. "I'll

talk to Leora myself, see if I can get her to withdraw her claim on Fiona."

"She won't. 'Tis obvious she's determined to have her." Was he blind, or did he really think he could talk sense into his sister?

"Have faith. Faith in God, faith in me, faith in the law."

"But sure, and when has the law been me friend? Or God for that matter. You, I'm still trying to decide on." He would be all too easy to trust. And she couldn't do that. Not yet. Hadn't he stood in her way every step she took? Yes, she was grateful for his intervention with God on Fiona's behalf. But good man or not, Sheriff Simon Masters was a force to be reckoned with. And Maggie didn't know how to handle him. It looked as if she would have plenty of time to learn, though.

"You never told me what Mrs. Watson said. You told her the truth, didn't you?"

"Aye. She was most gracious. But she says the same as you. Always trust God. But He hasn't proved He's trustworthy to me. He took me mum and fa. But for that, there would be no question of Fiona not staying with her own kin."

"This is something you'll have to work out, Maggie. I don't know all God's ways. The one thing I do know is that God loves you. He wants only the best for you. We don't see all He sees. But I know He's there for you if you'll open your eyes and look." He stepped away. "I'm going to arrange for our train tickets. You pack while I'm gone and dress in more appropriate clothing. I don't want anyone else in Wabash to know what happened. The last thing I want is for someone to press kidnapping charges."

"Kidnapping? Fiona is me own flesh and blood! If there was any kidnapping to be done, it was your sister who did it." Maggie's blood boiled at the outrage.

"Settle down. Just get packed and ready. Let's not borrow trouble."

"But sure, and trouble seems to follow me. I don't need to borrow any—'tis plenty of me own I have."

He grinned. "Things will look up when we least expect it, Maggie." Whistling, he went to the door and pulled it shut behind him.

"Humph! Easy for him to say." He wasn't the one whose entire future rested on the whim of the court. She knelt beside her trunk and pulled out a simple cotton dress. When she was clad in the dress, she stared at her reflection in the dim mirror on the dresser. A waif stared back at her. What judge in his right mind would award Fiona's care to someone who looked like that? She looked as if she needed someone to care for her as well as Fiona.

Maggie groaned. Why had she ever cut her hair? She looked plain without it. And she looked far younger than her seventeen years. But she'd been so sure they could escape as boys. And they would have but for the meddling sheriff. Her shoulder still felt warm where he had held it. In spite of his meddling she liked him. No, she more than liked him. And that wasn't good. He was the enemy. She needed to remember that.

By the time Simon returned, Maggie was packed and ready. Simon's gaze flickered to her hair, and he grinned but didn't say anything. Maggie was grateful for that. She knew she looked plain and pitiful.

Simon hefted her small trunk to his shoulder. "This all you have?"

"But sure, and isn't it enough? Can I help you carry it?"

"It doesn't weigh much," he said. "You'll need to carry Fiona anyway. We have to hurry. The train is pulling out in twenty minutes."

Twenty minutes and they would be on their way back to Wabash. And Fiona wouldn't be with her any longer. Maggie knew this in her heart, for all the sheriff's optimistic words. The world hadn't shown itself to be a place worthy of that kind of optimism to Maggie. She picked up Fiona and followed Simon down the stairs.

Breathless from rushing along the streets, Maggie heard the train whistle shriek. Then the train barreled into the station, throwing cinders that burned her eyes and choked her throat. Blinking back the stinging debris, Maggie mounted the steps to the passenger car as though she were mounting the steps to the gallows.

She wished she could grab Fiona and rush away in the throng where no one could find them. She steadied herself with a hand on the railing and entered the train car with dignity. She had no other choice. Being tracked down like a criminal had been humiliating enough. Simon wouldn't hesitate to arrest her in front of this crowd.

The trip back seemed to take forever with the numerous stops along the way. When they pulled into the Wabash train station, Maggie wished it could have gone on much longer. She wasn't ready to face the town.

But as Simon helped her from the train, no one seemed to take much note of the runaway being hauled back unceremoniously. Simon hired a wagon, tossed her chest in the back, and drove the two girls up Wabash Street to Hill Street. He stopped in front of a large brick home with a tower that overlooked the town below.

"This is it." He dropped the reins and bounded to the ground, then held up his arms to help her down.

Maggie hated to let him. She had become angrier as they drove away from her little home on Miami Street. Couldn't he at least allow her to spend the first night in her own home? The man was an *eejit!* She wasn't going to run away again. But she supposed she couldn't fault him for fearing she might. She hadn't proven herself trustworthy, as he said.

His broad hands against her waist sent a flutter through her. Setting her on the ground, he held her a trifle longer than necessary. His breath ruffled her shorn hair, and a look of concern flickered in his eyes as he stared down at her.

"You're spitting mad at me, aren't you?" he asked.

He grinned as though he didn't mind, and all the warm, fuzzy thoughts Maggie had been feeling vanished. "But sure, and why wouldn't I be? You haul me across the state as though I'm a criminal, then don't even let me stay in me own dear wee house. You have no right to force me to stay here." She burst into tears. Embarrassed at her display, she sniffed and searched for her handkerchief. Turning her head, she presented her stiff back to him.

"Here." He thrust a handkerchief into her hand. "You don't give your trust easily, do you, Maggie? Prickly as a cactus, too. Don't you see that you have a better chance to get Fiona if you're under my mother's protection?"

She took his handkerchief and blew her nose.

"Why are you crying, Maggie?" Fiona tugged at her hand. "Don't you want to stay with Grammy?"

Grammy? Where had that come from? Maggie narrowed her eyes and glared at Simon. His sister again probably.

He shrugged. "Don't look at me. I didn't start that."

Maggie sniffed again and scooped up Fiona in her arms. "Of course I do," she declared loudly for Simon's benefit. "I was just sad for a minute and missing our house by the canal. Let's go see, er, Grammy."

Simon held open the door, and she swept inside with Fiona in her arms. He shut the door behind them with a solid thump that echoed through the entry. Abigail Masters came hurrying through a door almost as soon as the thump faded away.

"There you are!" she cried.

Maggie found herself enveloped by a warm embrace. The scent of rose sachet slipped up Maggie's nose in a comforting aroma of welcome. She hugged the woman back, then stepped out of the embrace. She would do well to remember this woman was as much the enemy as Simon. They were all after Fiona. She resolved to stay on her guard.

Her black dress covered by a snowy apron, a maid of about twenty-five came from the dining room on the left.

"Sally, show our guests to their room, would you?" Mrs. Masters turned back to Maggie. "I've put you and Fiona together in a room with two other girls. They are about your age, Maggie. I thought you might make friends." She nodded. "You look as though you could use a friend, my dear."

Tears stung Maggie's eyes. There were no friends to be found here. She wanted to fling open the front door and dash away. But she forced herself to follow Sally up the stairs. Fiona clung to her hand as she chattered away about the nice furnishings. Sally showed them to a large room on the third floor. Two beds near the dormer windows were empty of personal items.

"These here are yer beds," Sally said. "The linens is downstairs on the second floor. I'll show you the linen closet so you can make 'em up. All the residents is expected to work. I reckon Miz Masters'll tell you what she expects from you tomorrow. Fer now, you can get yer bed made up. Dinner's at seven."

With that she left them, and Maggie surveyed her new home. She'd always wished for an attic bedroom under the eaves. It was clean and cozy with a braided rug on the floor and colorful flowered paper on the walls. The other girls she would share the room with were not in residence, and that was fine with Maggie. She wanted to have a chance to collect her thoughts.

She sighed and removed her hat. Dropping onto the edge of the bed, she drew Fiona onto her lap and rested her chin on the top of her sister's head. Maggie wished she could crawl into bed and pull the covers up over her head. Maybe when she woke up tomorrow, this would all be a bad dream. She and Fiona would be in their own home, she would be making a living, and no disapproving sheriff would be there to tell her she was an unfit guardian for Fiona.

ten

Women! They were the most illogical, infuriating creatures. Simon stomped past his mother into the parlor. He was only trying to help, to do the best he could in a bad situation. And what did he get for it? Kicked like a mangy dog.

"Would you like some tea, Dear?" Two children came running through the parlor. His mother stopped them. "Hattie, Michael, what have I told you about running in the house?"

Simon hid a grin at his mother's firm tone. He'd heard that often enough himself during his growing-up years. She ruled the household with a firm yet gentle hand. His smile faded. His father had been a different matter.

"We ain't s'posed to run," the little boy responded. Ducking his head, he scuffed one toe against the carpet.

"Then why were you disobeying?" The children gave no response, just more head-hanging and shamefaced expressions.

"We're sorry, Mama Abigail," the little girl said.

"Run along now," Abigail told the children. "And try to remember next time." A slight smile played along her lips.

"You love this job, don't you, Mother?"

"It's very fulfilling," his mother admitted. "And someone had to do something. I wish I had a bigger home and could take in more children. But I know Jesus sees the mite I can do and approves." She settled herself on the sofa, a flowered chintz that had seen better days. Her orphanage children were hard on furnishings. "Now why don't you tell me why you have that long face?"

Simon sat beside her, his knees nearly touching the table in front of the sofa. He was suddenly weary. "Maggie's none too happy with me."

"Neither is your sister. She thought you should have brought them back right away."

"Fiona was ill. And there were other complications. I'll deal with Leora."

His mother sighed. "Your sister has pinned all her happiness on that child. She refuses to listen to reason. I don't know what made her take to that particular child. I have others here who need a home as well. But she says Fiona is her 'child of the heart.' "

Simon sighed. How could he reach Leora? He'd promised Maggie to do all he could to keep Fiona with her. Leora had powerful friends on the court. His hands might be tied. He took off his hat and mopped the perspiration from his forehead. "I wish this heat and humidity would break. It's barely April."

"A storm's coming. Old Amos at Beitman and Wolf says we'll see a bad one tonight." His mother picked up a tray. "Have a cookie, Dear. I'll have Sally bring you some coffee."

"Thanks, but I'd better get to the office and check on things. I'll stop by later."

"Come for dinner. It might help ease things with Maggie and Fiona."

Simon nodded. "See you later." He kissed his mother's

rose-scented cheek and went to the door. Outside he felt as if he were stepping into a Turkish bath. The air looked strange, too. Kind of greenish. Old Amos was probably right. It looked as if a bad storm was brewing. To the southwest, thunderheads stacked up like towering mountains. He stepped up into the buckboard and took it back to the livery before walking to his office.

Sam Travis, the town's deputy, had his feet propped on the scarred desk when Simon walked in. A portly man of about fifty, his stomach hid his belt, but nothing hid the genial grin he always wore. "Hey, Boss, I was beginning to think you decided to run off with that purty little gal."

Simon shot him a warning glance, but Sam just grinned. "Just kidding, Sheriff." He swung his feet to the floor. "Been pretty quiet since you've been gone. Martin Van Meter went on a binge last night, and I have him in the slammer to sober up. The jail is empty except for him."

"Glad to hear it. All I want is some peace and quiet." Simon hung his hat on the rack and sat in the chair Sam had vacated for him.

Sam grinned again. "I take it that pretty filly was a handful. You have to drag her back here kicking and screaming, or did she come peaceable-like?"

"She was none too pleased to be found. Anyone ask where I was?"

Sam shrugged. "Some. I said you were out of town for a few days, like you told me. What's the big secret?"

"Maggie is young. I didn't want a youthful indiscretion to ruin her reputation. She and Fiona are at my mom's orphanage." He grimaced. "With her hair all shorn, people likely will figure it out. But I don't aim to help them with their gossip. Thanks for keeping it quiet."

"No problem. I'll mosey on home now that you're back. My wife will be surprised to have me home in time for supper." He ambled to the door. "Your sister stopped by this morning. She was squawking about charging the girl with breaking and entering. You probably have your hands full with her."

Simon leaned his head into his hands and groaned.

Sam laughed. "Just keeping you informed, Boss. See you tomorrow." He shut the door behind him.

Simon leaned back in his chair and laced his fingers at the back of his neck. He should probably go see Leora and try to calm her down. But what could he say to her to convince her to agree to leave Fiona at the orphanage? She had an injunction from the judge awarding her temporary custody. She wouldn't be easy to convince.

Thunder rumbled in the distance. Simon walked to the door and stepped outside. The sky was greenish-black in the southwest and bearing down on them. He would get drenched if he started for Leora's. The storm would delay any action on her part as well. Breathing a prayer of thankfulness at his reprieve, he went back inside the jail. He would get caught up on paperwork before supper. He had several hours, and it would be a welcome relief to focus on numbers and ledgers instead of figuring out women.

The day had darkened considerably by the time he finished his ledgers and put them away. He took out his pocket watch. Six o'clock. Just enough time to get cleaned up and over to his mother's. He climbed the stairs to his quarters on the second floor. After shaving, he slicked his hair back with bay rum and changed his clothes. Why was he getting so gussied up? After the way Maggie had glared at him, his stock was in the basement.

But that knowledge didn't seem to stop his heart from speeding up as he left the office and strode up Miami Street toward Hill. The threatening clouds towered ever higher, and the air was so thick he felt as if he were moving through warm molasses. Simon watched the storm with an anxious eye. He'd never seen the sky look quite like this. He turned on Hill Street and bounded up the steps to the porch of the orphanage. Inside, the house was filled with shrieks and squeals from upstairs.

Sally rushed by him, her hair hanging in wisps down her neck. She saw him and skidded to a halt, smoothing her hair down with hasty fingers. "My lands, Sheriff! Them children are in an uproar today."

"What's happened?"

Sally shook her head. "Michael found a snake and started chasing the girls with it. Then Rachel fell down the back stairway, and we had to call the doctor. It's gotten all the kids at sixes and sevens. And then the snake escaped."

"Need any help?"

"Oh, would you mind, Sheriff? And could you put yer star back on? That'll put the fear of God in them children. "

Simon didn't want to put the fear of God into them. He wanted to put love there instead. He ignored Sally's request about the star and followed her up the stairs. Five children were clustered in a circle staring at the floor on the landing. Peering around them to see what held their attention, he saw Michael's snake. It had slithered to the railing and lay curled around a rail.

The group was all girls, so no one was making a move to capture the creature. Walking softly so as not to frighten the snake or the children, he moved toward the coiled garter snake. Its tongue flickered, and one of the little girls screamed. Simon heard a thump on the stairs behind him, and Maggie ran into the hall. The snake shot away in a flurry of motion, and pandemonium broke out. The children ran in every direction as Maggie stood frozen in place.

Maggie screamed as the snake made its way toward her, sliding over her foot and coming to rest under her skirts. Her face white as parchment, she continued to scream. Simon hadn't realized she could become quite so hysterical.

In two strides Simon was at her side and swept her up into his arms. The snake, deprived of its hiding place, slithered under a nearby table. Maggie wrapped her arms around his neck and buried her face against his chest, shuddering convulsively.

Protective instincts Simon didn't even know he possessed welled up within him. "Shush, it's all right," he whispered. He rested his chin against her hair and carried her down the steps to the parlor.

She raised her head, and Simon felt bereft as she began to struggle to be put down. He realized he didn't want to put her down. The shock of that realization made him nearly drop her. Hastily he gathered his composure and set her on the sofa. His arms felt empty without her in them.

"Where's Fiona?" Her face was white, and tears hovered on the edges of her lashes.

"Land's sakes, what's all the commotion?" Simon's mother asked, entering the room.

"Fiona, where is she?" Maggie seemed to be getting more upset by the second.

"She's in the kitchen with Sally, Child. Settle down."

Abigail's calm words had an immediate effect. Maggie visibly relaxed. Her fingers played with the folds of her dress, and she glanced toward the staircase. "The snake—"

"I'll take care of it now." Simon took the steps two at a time. The children had all departed for safer realms. Simon shoved the table out of the way and found the small garter snake coiled against the wall. Holding it behind its head, he scooped it up and carried it down the stairs and outside. He released it in the garden, then started back inside. Pausing on the front step, he saw the storm was almost upon them.

Lightning flickered, and the smell of heat hovered in the air. It was going to be a bad one all right. He hurried into the house and shut the door behind him, glad to be in a sturdy house like this one. He pitied those in the shanties by the river. If there was much rain, he'd have to see to evacuating them.

Maggie had regained her composure when he returned to the parlor. She sat sipping tea with his mother. A bit pale, she inclined her head to Simon.

"Thank you," she said quietly.

Simon frowned. He much preferred her anger to this polite coldness. But he guessed he couldn't blame her. Her whole life had turned upside down, and it was all because of him. He sat in the armchair by the fireplace and poured a cup of coffee from the tray on the table.

Sally thrust her head into the parlor. "Dinner is ready, Mrs. Masters."

"Thank you, Sally." She rose and moved toward the dining room.

The children came clattering down the steps. The snake scare had subdued them, and they kept their gazes fixed somewhere near the floor. Simon counted twenty children. The most his mother had ever cared for. The long dining room table would be full tonight. And for many nights to come.

Thunder shook the house, and the gaslights over the table flickered as the wind blew through the cracks around the windows. Maggie gasped and clasped her arms around herself. "But sure, and I hate storms."

Simon wanted to gather her back into his arms and comfort her, but he merely held out a chair for her. The thunder rattled again. She blanched and sank onto the chair.

"This hasn't been a good day for you," he murmured.

She glared at him. Ah, there was the old Maggie, full of vinegar. "I'm not the enemy, you know," he whispered. "I'm on your side."

"We'll see what you say when your sister shows up to take Fiona." She fluffed her napkin and laid it on her lap.

Frustration rose in his throat. He was tired of being the responsible one, tired of the burden of the town, the burden of his family. But there was no one else to shoulder it. And it was his anyway. As much as he wished to be free of it, he would never let someone else carry it. He had to figure out some way to guide them all through this mess. And when this was over, maybe he could court Maggie. He bit the corner of his lip to keep from grinning. He must be mad. She wouldn't have him on a silver platter. Not after this.

Dinner was a strange affair with thunder rumbling around the house so loudly that polite conversation was impossible. The wind howled through the eaves, and buckets of rain pummeled the house and sluiced down the windows.

They had finished the meal when a strange shaking seemed to seize the house. A sound like a train roared over their heads.

It was a familiar sound to Simon. He leapt to his feet. "It's a tornado! Get to the basement!" he shouted. He grabbed Maggie's hand and swept Fiona up with the other arm. The house trembled again, and windows began to blow out as they all stumbled toward the basement stairs.

The children began to shriek and run from the room. Abigail carried a lamp and guided the children as best she could with Sally's help. Simon knew the children were screaming because he could see their open mouths, but the noise of the storm drowned out their cries. He held open the basement door, and the children hurried down the steps one by one with his mother leading the way with the lamp.

He turned to look behind him and saw pieces of glass blowing past. Slamming the basement door, he rushed down the steps. The roars echoing from the upstairs sounded as though the storm were devouring the house. Glass shattering, furniture scraping across the floor, and the wind howling.

With his heart pounding, Simon began to pray aloud

for their safety. His words calmed the children; they drew close to him and bowed their heads. He crouched on the floor with his arms around Maggie and Fiona. Maggie had apparently forgotten her animosity, for she clung to him. Fiona burrowed against his other side, and Simon was strangely content in the midst of the storm. God was here in this place with them.

The storm seemed to go on forever. When it was finally over, the ensuing silence echoed almost as loudly. Simon reluctantly let go of his two charges and stared at the rest of the basement's inhabitants. "Everyone all right?" They all looked shaken. He knew he probably looked as rattled as they did.

His mother drew a shuddering breath. "Is there anything left of our home, Simon?" Her voice trembled.

"I'll see. You all stay here until I check out what's happened."

"I'm going with you." Maggie scrambled to her feet.

"No, you're not. I don't know what's up there." But he was afraid it was not going to be good.

"But sure, and you'll not be going up there alone." Maggie gathered her skirts in her hand and moved toward him.

The determination on her face told him he wouldn't sway her. "Very well," he said. "But mind where you step." He took her hand and led her up the stairs. Pushing open the door, they stepped into what was left of the hall. Simon's heart came up into his throat.

The tornado had blown through the house leaving devastation in its wake. The windows were blown out; the furniture had been tossed against the walls and broken into pieces. Water drenched the carpets and hardwood floors. But the brick home was still standing. Simon knew it was a miracle. But his mother would be crushed at the destruction of her belongings.

"But sure, and we must check out the upstairs." Maggie moved past him to the stairs.

He grabbed her arm. "Wait! It might not be safe. I'd better go first."

" 'Tis not a child I am, Sheriff." She tossed her head and pulled away. "Me belongings are up there on the attic floor."

He moved past her. "I'm going first."

He mounted the steps cautiously and stopped on the second-floor landing. The same devastation met his gaze. While he stood there dazed by what he saw, Maggie started climbing the stairs to the attic. He rushed after her. The wind brushed his face as his head reached the top of the steps. The roof was gone, and rain poured down upon them.

The third floor was swept clean of all but the bare floorboards. Still on the steps with only their heads above the third floor, Simon felt Maggie sway, and he put an arm around her.

She buried her face in her hands and burst into tears. " 'Tis gone, all of it. All I've worked for these past years. All me savings, even me mum's trunk with her wedding dress in it." She turned to Simon for comfort. His arms closed around her, and he wished he could take this pain from her and make it his own instead.

eleven

Her shoulders slumped, Maggie followed Simon down the steps. Gone, all of it. Fiona's clothing, her few battered toys, the chest that had belonged to their mum with the few precious possessions left to them by their parents. How could she bear this loss? For there was no doubt Fiona would be taken from her now. What could she possibly offer a child? No belongings, no home, no longer any job. They were destitute.

Tears burned in her eyes, and she wanted to cry. She clenched her jaw and fought for control. Weeping would not change the circumstances.

Simon's fingers were warm and strong as he took her hand to assist her. His gaze locked with hers, and the sympathy in his eyes battered down her defenses. A sob rose in her throat.

He brushed her chin with the back of his hand. "I'm sorrier than I can say," he said softly. "I wish I could stay, but there's no telling what's happening in the town. We could have injured people or some trapped in the rubble."

She held back her tears and nodded. He was right. For a moment she forgot her personal losses. Others might be less fortunate. She straightened her shoulders. "But sure, and I'll come with you. You will need all the help you can get."

"Mother needs help here, too. I don't know what we can do about the children. We need to find a shelter for them and for others who have lost their homes."

They both turned as Simon's mother pushed open the door from the basement and led the children out of the dark dampness below. Abigail stopped in her tracks and looked around at what had been an elegant home a few moments before.

"Oh dear." She put her hand to her throat. "My lovely things." Her gaze wandered around the room. The color drained from her face, and she swayed, then reached out a hand to the wall to steady herself.

Maggie saw tears in her eyes, but Abigail did not let them fall. "We must thank the good Lord that no children were injured," she said softly.

The children were somber and subdued as they filed behind the older woman into the hall. Several of the little girls began to cry, and Fiona ran to Maggie. Lifting her in her arms, Maggie comforted her. But she longed for some comfort herself. What little she had possessed was gone. The storm had changed everything.

Maggie swallowed the lump in her throat. "We must find a place for the children tonight. I'm going with Simon to see what can be done." She turned to Sally. "You see what you can do about finding someone to board up the windows in the parlor and the kitchen. But sure, and I'll be back as quick as I can." She set Fiona on the floor. "You be good, me girl. Pay attention to Sally."

Fiona threw herself against Maggie's legs and cried, "I want to stay with you!"

Maggie smoothed back her hair. "I'm leaving you in charge of the little children, Fiona. They are depending on you."

Fiona's tears dried instantly, and she stared at the two children who were even younger than she. Her lower lip still protruded, but she nodded and moved toward them.

Maggie breathed a sigh of relief and took Simon's arm. The admiration in his gaze warmed her. She couldn't do anything to help herself, but she could help the others in the town. Simon's warm fingers closed over her hand as he squeezed it.

"Let's go," she said.

They stepped through the battered doorway onto the porch. Though the milky twilight dimmed the scene, it was obvious the town had been hit hard. Tree limbs littered the streets, and the shattered hulks of houses shocked Maggie further. Was there anything left of her little home? She held to Simon's arm as they picked their way through the debris and walked down Wabash Street toward the courthouse.

Tree limbs and other debris littered the boardwalk and corduroy road, but it looked as if the downtown businesses had escaped the worst of the storm's fury. A crowd was gathering in front of the courthouse by the time they arrived.

"The mayor's out of town," Simon whispered to Maggie. "So I guess the responsibility for the town falls on my shoulders."

"But sure, and I can think of no one else better to shoulder it," Maggie whispered back. He squeezed her hand in reply, and a tide of warmth spread over her cheeks. She was relieved the twilight hid her blush. Why did he affect her like this? He was the enemy, but she couldn't seem to remember that.

"There's the sheriff!" The murmur swept through the crowd. People covered in mud and debris, wearing expressions of shock and dismay, turned toward them.

Simon held up his hands. "We've got a long night ahead of us, folks. Is everyone accounted for? Do we know of anyone who is missing?"

Some nodded and spoke among themselves, but no one called out the names of missing loved ones. Maggie felt the tension in Simon ease a bit.

"How many of you have your houses fairly intact? We're going to need places for others to stay. My mother's house is pretty damaged, and she's going to need some help with the children."

Several people held up their hands, and Simon soon had housing arranged for those who had lost their homes.

"Tomorrow we're going to start the cleanup, so you'd all better get some rest. I'll be at the jail all night. If you have any problems, come and see me there." Simon dismissed the crowd and took hold of Maggie's hand again.

The camaraderie of holding hands with the sheriff seemed so natural in that moment. It was as if the storm had blown away the tension between them and replaced it with something else. Maggie wasn't sure what to call that something. Affection? Or maybe cautious trust? Whatever it was, it left her feeling uncertain but happy. Happy in spite of having lost all her money and possessions. She started to examine where that happiness had come from but decided it might vanish if she gave it a name. And if there was one thing the O'Keefes knew about, it was the way happiness could turn in your hand and become tragedy.

Maggie mingled with the crowd, getting names of those who would take some of the children. The women seemed to cling to her, to want to share their experiences with her. She listened and shook her head in dismay at the stories, which seemed to be all the women needed. Warmed by the feeling that she had been able to help, she finally found her way back to Simon's side.

"I'll walk you to Mother's," Simon said. He clasped her hand, and they walked back toward the house in companionable silence. "Thanks for coming with me, Maggie. You're a remarkable young woman. Most women would have been cowering at home after what you've been through tonight."

Maggie swallowed hard. "But sure, and me father always said I was a nosy one. I wanted to see what was going on."

"You can laugh all you want, but I know it was because you care about other people." He pressed her hand, then drew it to his lips.

The touch of his warm lips against the back of her hand did strange things to Maggie's breathing. There was no future in her feeling this way, but she couldn't seem to help herself. She was a nobody, a waif with no home and no future; but walking beside Simon, she felt as though she could do anything.

"Can you see to delivering the children to the people who offered to take them?" Simon asked as they paused outside the door to his mother's orphanage.

"But sure, and who else is there?" Maggie smiled up at Simon. "And what will you be doing while I'm working me fingers to the bone?"

He chuckled. "Doing the same. I'm going to take a walk through town and see if I can offer any assistance before I go to my office. I'll be back first thing in the morning, though."

"I'll be at me house on Miami Street. And your mother, too, if she cares to stay with me. There're a few extra beds as well as floor space with blankets for some of the children."

He squeezed her hand again. "I'm sure she'll be touched by your offer." He stood staring down at her.

The moment seemed to draw out between them, and Maggie felt connected to Simon in a way she'd never felt with anyone before. She stared up at him nervously. What was he thinking? Had his views of her altered at all? Something had changed tonight.

Simon raised his hand and cupped her cheek in his palm. "You're so lovely, Maggie. Shorn hair and all."

Maggie caught her breath at his touch. Her heart jolted against her ribs in sudden awareness. Then Simon bent his head, and his lips claimed hers. Maggie closed her eyes as dizziness swept over her. She clung to Simon as waves of emotion swept her away in a maelstrom of love. That's what she felt toward Simon. Love. Until this moment she hadn't wanted to admit, even to herself, that love was what she felt when she looked into his eyes.

He began to draw away, and she threw her arms around his neck, holding him for a moment longer. His arms drew her close again, and his kiss deepened in fervor. With a muffled cry, Maggie realized how wanton she must seem. She pulled herself away, though her limbs felt as though they couldn't hold her.

Simon's gaze was tender as he looked into her face. Maggie tore herself free from his arms. "I must be getting inside. Your mum will wonder what's become of us. And the children need care." Maggie was consumed with shame. She'd thrown herself at him. He'd meant a friendly kiss, nothing more, and she'd turned it into something else. Her eyes burned with the enormity of her actions.

"Maggie, wait!"

But she didn't wait. She couldn't bear to see the look on his face. What must he think of her? She threw open the door and stumbled inside. Her face burned. Why had she acted in such a fashion? But she'd been helpless to show her love for him with the realization of her feelings so fresh. She knew he must have been shocked. Shocked and disgusted at her behavior.

She swallowed and smoothed back her hair. Forcing a smile, she went in search of the others. Abigail and Sally had gathered all the children in the parlor. Several were playing pick-up sticks while Abigail read a story by lamplight to another group.

Fiona jumped up when Maggie came into the parlor. "What took you so long?" she cried.

Maggie scooped her up and hugged her. "I wasn't gone long."

"You look funny, Maggie," Fiona said. "Your face is red. Was it sad to see all the houses broken?"

"This is one of the worst," Maggie said.

Abigail laid the book aside. "Come and sit down, my dear. You must be exhausted. Was anyone hurt by the storm?"

"I don't think so. Nothing major anyway. We found housing for everyone. Mrs. Carpenter will take six children, the Merriweathers will take four, and I think there's room for the rest at me own house, if you'd like to stay there. I have plenty of blankets to make pallets on the floor for the children. There are two beds in Fiona's room, and she can sleep with me." She was thankful the house had come furnished, for she would not have wasted the money on extra beds and bedding.

"Excellent! Thank you most kindly, dear Maggie."

Maggie could feel the woman's speculative gaze on her, and she turned away. "Let's be off then before it gets any darker. There is much debris, and the walking will be difficult."

Maggie rose and took one-year-old Will in her arms. Sally picked up two-year-old Callie. The rest of the children lined up behind Abigail and followed them out into the street. The storm had left a blast of cold air in its wake, and Maggie shivered, wishing her wool shawl hadn't been blown away.

The Carpenters and the Merriweathers lived on Main Street. Their houses appeared almost untouched, and they seemed glad to take the children when the little parade stopped at their homes. Maggie found it hard to keep her thoughts away from Simon's kiss as she led the rest of the ragtag group toward her house.

How would she face Simon tomorrow? Her face still burned with the shame of her actions. She pushed the thought away and walked up onto her porch. Opening the door, she lit the lamp inside while the rest of the group filed in. She directed them to the rooms upstairs, then lit a fire in the stove.

It felt so good to be home. But how long would she be allowed to stay? The future was so uncertain. At least for now she didn't have to think about tomorrow, didn't have to worry about the court or the law. Nothing would be done until the town recovered from the storm. The reprieve wouldn't last, but it was better than nothing.

The next morning the cold air blowing in around the windows awakened Maggie. She lay for a moment in the soft bed. With Fiona curled beside her, she could almost imagine life was as it had been a month ago. It seemed an eternity ago. Everything was so right then. Her business was growing, and they had money enough for the necessities and even money enough to save. But the little she had saved was gone.

In determination she rose. She could bake this morning. Maybe some of her customers would smell the bread and pies and come to purchase them. It was a start. She might not be allowed to continue, but every nickel she earned was one she didn't have to take from charity. Maggie pulled on her dress and shoes, then tiptoed down the steps. It was only five. Let the others sleep as long as they could. They were all exhausted from the stress.

By the time Abigail came yawning down the steps at eight, Maggie had baked a half-dozen loaves of bread, cinnamon rolls, and two pies. She'd sold all but the cinnamon rolls, saving them for her guests' breakfast.

"That smells wonderful," Abigail said. She sat at the table and watched Maggie work. "You're very good at that. I see no reason why you shouldn't continue your business when things return to normal. You could spend the nights with us at the orphanage."

Maggie kept her head down. It was kind of her to offer that, but she wasn't the one in control of the courts.

"That upsets you?"

Maggie raised her eyes and met the older woman's gaze. "But sure, and I can't help but hope that Fiona and I will soon be allowed to take care of ourselves in our own home."

Abigail was quiet for a moment. "I understand, my dear. But you must face facts. If you want to get Fiona back, we must do all we can to ensure the court awards you custody."

Maggie began to pummel the bread. "But sure, and I have no choice now, do I? But I'll earn my keep while I'm there. For me and Fiona."

"That's all I ask," Abigail said. "May I?" She inclined her head toward the cinnamon rolls.

" 'Tis what I made them for," Maggie said. "I made plenty for the children as well." The rest of the children trooped down the steps and soon devoured the cinnamon rolls.

Maggie untied her apron and hung it on the peg by the stove. "I should see if there's anything to be done in the town. Have I your permission to see if I can be of service?"

Abigail looked at her. "I'm not your enemy, Maggie. I'm on your side," she said softly. "And I'd like us to be friends."

Shame filled Maggie. She had no reason to take her frustration out on the woman. She was just trying to help. It wasn't her fault that Leora was trying to take Fiona. "I'm sorry," she said. "But sure, and I know you're not the enemy. But 'tis hard when I've been on me own for these three years."

Abigail laid her hand on Maggie's arm. "Just give me a chance, Maggie. That's all I ask. And Simon. He's trying so hard to work this out for the best."

Maggie didn't doubt that. But sometimes all the trying in the world did nothing. She didn't want to think about Simon. And the thought of facing him this morning made her mouth go dry. But it had to be faced. And Fa always said that when something was hard, it didn't get easier by avoiding it. She squared her shoulders and went to the door. She might as well get it over with.

twelve

Simon rubbed his burning eyes. He'd had no sleep last night, but it wasn't due to the storm. The memory of Maggie's response drove all exhaustion from him. What was he going to do about her? He was the law in this town. It was his duty to see justice carried out, but did justice include ripping her family apart because she was young or ignoring the powerful emotions she evoked in him?

Simon raked his fingers through his hair. Tossing the questions around in his mind brought him no closer to a resolution about what to do. Did Maggie really care about him, or was she hoping she could turn him from his duty with a display of affection? He found it hard to believe that of her, but how well did he know her? Until she returned his kiss with such eagerness, he never would have guessed she held any feelings for him beyond contempt.

Muttering, he shoved himself away from his desk and stood. Enough of this soul-searching. He had work to do. It was light enough now to see the full extent of the damage the storm had left. Work would get his mind off Maggie. Besides, he was a sheriff, not a do-gooder who enjoyed sticking his nose in other people's business. He pulled on a coat and strode out the door.

A heavy frost from last night covered the trees, and Simon's breath fogged in the cool air. Wabash still slept, exhausted from the turmoil of the previous evening, no doubt. Not even the café had opened for breakfast yet this morning. But he could smell something baking. His mouth watered at the scent of cinnamon rolls. Where was that aroma coming from? The only other place in town—he stopped at the thought. *Maggie. She must be up and baking already this morning.*

He could buy breakfast there. His mouth went dry at the thought of seeing her. He didn't know what to do about her.

The rattle of a buckboard drew his attention, and he turned. His heart sank when he saw Leora's intent face. Everett guided the horse to a stop and jumped down. He helped his wife to the ground, and they both approached Simon.

"I heard you found them!" Leora said breathlessly. Her eyes were bright. "Where is Fiona?"

"She's with Maggie."

Leora's brows drew together. "You let her stay with that kidnapper? How could you? You should have brought her directly to me."

"The child is still recovering from her bout with pneumonia, Leora. We were all tired from the train trip as well. They were safely housed at Mother's."

"I'll go home and get her then."

"She's not there any longer; they're at Maggie's house. And Mother as well."

That stopped Leora. "What's happened?"

"Didn't you get the storm? A tornado came through town last night. The roof is gone on Mother's house, and the other floors are severely damaged. We had too much glass and destruction to stay there last night. Mother and all the children will need a place to stay for several weeks while the house is rebuilt."

Leora's mouth dropped open, and she covered it with her hand. "Oh, no! Was anyone hurt?"

"Nothing serious, just a few cuts from flying glass." *At least she is concerned about something besides taking possession of Fiona,* Simon thought grimly.

"I need to see Mother. I could take a couple of children," Leora said. "Even with Fiona, I have room."

"About Fiona, Leora," Simon began.

She held up a hand. "Don't even start, Simon. The judge awarded me temporary custody, and if I have to go back to court to make you do your duty, I'll do it. And what you and everyone else in this family fail to see is that something has knit that child into my heart. Fiona—not just any little waif, though you know I love children. But Fiona is special. I knew that the first time I looked in her eyes."

"I want you to think about Fiona instead of what you want."

Leora's eyes narrowed. "If her sister is such a good caretaker, why did she steal Fiona out of her sickbed?"

Simon had no answer for that. He hunched his shoulders and shrugged. "Maggie loves her sister. It's ripping both of them apart to know they can't be a family any longer."

"Hello, Leora, Simon." Maggie's voice broke the tension between Simon and Leora.

How long had she been standing there? What had she heard? Simon cleared his throat. "Hello, Maggie." His gaze was caught by her green eyes. His heart did a maddening clatter against his rib cage. Foolish, that's what he was.

"I've come for Fiona," Leora said.

Simon saw Maggie's throat move convulsively as she swallowed hard. She inclined her head. "She's at our home with your mother."

"I'll gather her and her things then." Leora turned toward the buckboard. She paused beside Maggie, and her face softened. "I'm sorry this is hurting you, Maggie. Truly I am. But I feel in my heart this is for the best. We can give Fiona a happy home. She's already part of our family in some almost miraculous way. Can't you at least try to consider not fighting this?"

Everett touched her arm. "Perhaps we should check with the doctor, Leora, and see if he thinks Fiona is in good enough health to be moved again."

Leora hesitated, then nodded. "I wouldn't want to do anything to hurt her." She turned back to Maggie. "Please, Maggie, it would be best if we could try to be friends."

Maggie blanched and pressed her lips together. *No doubt to keep the hot words from spilling out,* Simon thought. Maggie was not one to give up.

"Would you be agreeable for Maggie to visit whenever she wants?" Simon asked.

Leora blinked, and her mouth turned down. After a slight pause, she nodded. "It would be best for Fiona, I'm sure, to have her sister come to see her. I don't want to take your place, Maggie. I want to be her mother, and Everett wants to be her father. You will always be her sister."

"You both talk as if I'll be giving up me sister without a fight." Maggie's eyes began to spark with outrage. "But sure, and I should never have taken her that way when she was sick. But she is me sister, and we belong together. I'll not run from a fight again. I will fight you, Leora. You'll not take her easily."

Leora set her mouth in a firm line. "Very well. A fight you shall have. But I intend to win." She walked off with Everett close behind her. He helped her into the buckboard, and she stared down at them. "We will get the doctor and see you at your house."

They drove away in a clatter and parked the buckboard in front of the doctor's office. Simon turned back to Maggie. "I'm sorry. Legally there's nothing I can do. She has the law on her side right now."

Maggie pressed a hand to her forehead. "But sure, and I know that, Simon. 'Tis grateful I am that you want to help. But I must fight her somehow. You know the law. Is there anything I can do?"

"I'll have to study up on it, Maggie," he admitted. "I know more about robbery and other felony laws. But my closest friend is a lawyer. I'll see if there's anything he can suggest."

" 'Tis grateful I am, Simon, for your friendship." Maggie pressed her hand against his arm. "I—I want you to know that last night—" She stopped and swallowed hard.

Simon studied her face. Disappointment flooded him. Maybe she was sorry she'd kissed him. He wasn't sorry, not one bit. Just confused over how she felt. And how he felt. "We'd better go meet Leora and the doctor at your house. I'm not going to apologize for last night, if that's what you're asking for. I'm sorry if I upset you." He offered her his arm for support, and she laid her fingers on his forearm.

Her face flamed with color, and Simon knew she didn't want to talk about last night any more than he did. Maybe they were both confused. He certainly was.

When they arrived at Maggie's, Abigail was seated at the kitchen table with the children. "There you are, Simon. I was about to send Sally out to look for you. Have you been by the house in the daylight? I need to see about arranging for a carpenter to repair it. We cannot impose on Maggie any longer than necessary. Perhaps we should even see about renting a house?"

"There's no need for that," Maggie put in hastily. " 'Tis glad I am to have you here."

Abigail smiled and patted Maggie's hand. "You're a good girl, Maggie O'Keefe."

Color flooded Maggie's cheeks. She looked beautiful to Simon, even with her ragged haircut. He hoped her hair would grow quickly, though. He would like to see that glorious red hair down on her shoulders. He pushed such thoughts away and turned toward the door at the sound of a knock.

Opening the door, he stepped aside to let Leora and Everett enter with the doctor. When Fiona saw Leora, she ran to her. Leora's eyes grew bright as she scooped the little girl up into her arms. Whatever her faults, there was no doubt Leora truly cared about the child. Simon had to admit that. And it was obvious Fiona liked her. That was dangerous. The judge might take that into consideration.

Leora carried Fiona to the table and sat on a chair with the little girl in her lap. Simon hated to see the look of suffering on Maggie's face as she watched her sister with Leora. There seemed to be no way out of this mess. Or if there was, he didn't see it now.

"Let's take a look at this little lady." The doctor set his bag on the table and took out his stethoscope. Fiona giggled when he placed it against her chest.

The doctor listened intently, then smiled. "Nothing wrong with those lungs, my girl. You sure you had pneumonia a few days ago?"

"She was very sick," Maggie put in. "But Simon prayed for her, and God made her well."

"God can fix things I can't touch." The doctor put his stethoscope away and stood. "I'd better get back to my office."

Simon saw him to the door. His heart was heavy as he thought of Maggie's grief. But he couldn't do anything.

Leora smiled. "Let's get your things together, Fiona. You're coming home with me and Everett."

Fiona's mouth puckered. "Can Maggie come, too?"

Leora pressed her lips together. "Come along, Darling. Your dolly is waiting for you in your room." She struggled to hold onto Fiona. "Get her things," she told Maggie.

Maggie's eyes flooded with tears, but she didn't argue. She left the room, and Simon heard her climb the stairs. Even her steps sounded defeated. He clenched his fists at his side. For the first time in his life, he questioned his calling to be a sheriff. He'd always thought this was what God wanted him to do with his life. But now he had to wonder. The law was one thing, but justice seemed to be something else entirely in this case. Would there be justice for his Maggie? His Maggie. He gulped at the thought. What was he thinking?

Fiona was still crying for Maggie when she returned, but she was empty-handed. "But sure, and I don't know what I was thinking," she said. "She has no belongings. We lost everything in the storm."

Leora's eyes widened. "No clothes, nothing?"

"Just the clothes on her back."

Leora looked at Everett. She stood up and handed Fiona to him. Fiona kicked and screamed, holding out her arms for Maggie. "Come along, then. We'll pick up some clothes for her on our way out of town."

Maggie reached over and kissed her little sister. "Be good, Fiona," she whispered. "I'll be getting you back soon—don't fear."

"Leora, I must say I'm ashamed of you," Abigail finally said. "You're not thinking of this child at all."

Her chin thrust out, Leora looked at her mother and stalked to the door. "You've never understood me, Mother. I don't know why I expected this time to be any different. The law has more faith in me than you do." Everett followed her through the door with the screaming child.

Simon began to wonder at the situation. Maybe Leora was right, and they were all wrong. What she had said on the street made sense. Fiona would have a mother and a father who loved her. Maggie would still be around as her sister. He glanced at Maggie. Her face was a mask of suffering, and all his rational thoughts disintegrated.

Even with the door shut, they could hear Fiona's wails down the street. Abigail pressed her hand to her eyes. "I'm sorry, Maggie," she said. "Sorrier than I can say.

You probably rue the day you met this family."

"But sure, and 'tis not your fault, Abigail," Maggie said. " 'Tis my mistake that has brought this to pass. But hard it is to have Fiona suffer for me own error."

Simon knew he had to do something. He couldn't stand around this kitchen hoping Maggie would get Fiona back. Right or wrong, he would have to figure out a way to help it along. He would try to get Fiona back for Maggie; and if they didn't succeed, then God had other plans. He cared about Maggie in ways he wasn't willing to examine too closely. Her pain was his. In a sudden decision, he clapped his hat on his head and went to the door.

"I'll be back later. I have some business to attend to." He strode out the door and walked to Market Street. Robert Mitchell should be in his law office by now. Simon's steps quickened. His friend would know what to do to help Maggie. If Simon had to pay for the help out of his own pocket, he would do so willingly.

The Mitchell law office was a small room above the millinery shop on Market Street. Dust motes danced in the sunshine streaming through the glass windows that fronted the office. Robert was alone, and for that Simon was grateful. He couldn't have sat and waited if his life depended on it. He wanted to do something and do it now.

Robert smiled and stretched when he saw Simon. They'd gone to school together, but every time Simon saw him, he wondered where that carefree young boy had gone. Now Robert sported a beard and a belly as portly as his own father's. Simon saw no trace of the kid who used to dunk him in the old swimming hole.

Robert held out his hand. "Hey, old buddy, I was just

thinking about you. Quite a storm we had last night, wasn't it? I saw the damage to your mother's house. How is she taking the shock?"

Simon shook Robert's outstretched hand. "She's fine. I need to talk to you."

Robert's eyebrows lifted. "Sounds serious. Have a seat." He indicated the chair opposite his desk.

Simon sat, then leaned forward. "I have a friend in trouble, Robert. You know much about family law?"

He laughed. "That *is* my job, Simon. What's the problem?"

"Whatever you charge, I'll pay. This friend, Maggie O'Keefe, is only seventeen. She's been caring for her little sister for three years." He took off his hat and raked his hand through his hair. "It's all my fault, really. The little girl wandered away from the house while Maggie's back was turned. She was missing for two days, and when she was discovered, she was bruised and scratched. I had no way of knowing whether the sister was a fit caregiver at first. I had no choice but to try to uphold the law. Anyway, my sister found the little girl and is trying to keep her. I've since realized Maggie is as good a caregiver as any mother. But a judge awarded Leora temporary custody, and she's going to try to adopt Fiona permanently. What can I do to help Maggie keep her?"

Robert stroked his whiskered chin. "This is a sticky problem, Simon. Twenty-one is the legal age, you know. There isn't much that can be done to stop it. Unless someone else would ask to adopt Fiona, then have Maggie live there as well. What about your mother?"

It was a thought. But he shook his head. "She wouldn't

want to alienate Leora. She is her mother, too, after all."

"Pity. Then she should resign herself to simply staying in touch with her sister. That's the best I can offer." He fell silent, then narrowed his eyes. "There is one other thought."

"Yes?" Simon said eagerly.

"She could marry. That would change everything. The court would be reluctant to pull the child from a stable home, and her husband would have legal custody."

The thought of Maggie marrying someone else made Simon shudder. Then his eyes widened. He could marry her himself. At the thought, his heart began to pound. Marriage was a big step. And God wouldn't approve of a marriage made only to let Maggie keep Fiona. Besides, Maggie wasn't a believer. But the thought, once born, wouldn't go away.

Simon rose and clapped Robert on the back. "Thanks, my friend. I'll think about what you've said and see what can be done."

"If you have any other questions, just stop by." Robert walked him to the door.

Simon nodded and went down the steps to the street. His interfering was bound to bring more trouble on his head from his family. Leora wouldn't appreciate his interfering, and neither would his mother. He was more confused than when he had come. At times like these, God's Word didn't seem to understand a man's predicament, but Simon had to remember the reasons for His laws. Thinking about it rationally, he knew marriage wasn't an option, not to an unbeliever; but what did he do with the way this woman drew him?

thirteen

Maggie couldn't bear to sit and listen to the children play in the kitchen. She went to her room and shut the door. Fiona was gone, and she had a feeling she would never again tuck her sister into bed or read her a bedtime story. Leora had won. But Maggie couldn't even find the heart to hate her. Leora truly loved Fiona—that much was obvious.

What was she going to do now? She could indenture herself to someone; that was allowed by law for a minor. But it felt wrong to do that after she'd had control of her own life so long. And who would take her? Everyone would take one look at her shorn hair and wonder what she'd done. The questions would follow. She would be allowed to have her bakery business; Simon's mother had been clear about that. But could she stay here? She didn't have enough money now to move away and start a business somewhere else. It was either stay here and make the best of it or try to start fresh making a pittance as a shop girl or a seamstress.

She wanted to stay in her room, to shut out the world and all its problems. She sat in the rocker and stared out on the street. But she didn't really see the storm-littered streets still being pummeled with rain. Her misery was too profound.

She heard a knock at the door. She was tempted not to

answer it; maybe whoever it was would go away. But the knock sounded again, and she sighed and smoothed the sides of her hair back. "Come in."

The door opened slowly, and Abigail thrust her head inside the room. "We have too much work to do for you to be up here brooding, Maggie. Come along, and we'll get started cleaning up my house. Sally will stay here with the children and keep them occupied. But I need your help."

Maggie kept her head down. The last thing she wanted to do was to go back to that house and be reminded of all she'd lost. Self-pity was much more appealing.

The older woman's tone brooked no opposition. "We have no time to waste. Come along, Child."

Maggie jerked her head up. "I'm not a child! I'm a woman grown! Why can't all of you understand that? Even Simon—" Her voice faltered.

Abigail stepped farther into the room. "Simon what? I've seen the way you look at him. And the way he looks at you. He knows you're a woman, Maggie. And I know it, too. Maybe something will blossom between you. But you have to reach down and find that old fire you had. You can't stay up here in your room and ignore the life you could have."

"Me family is gone now," Maggie said softly. "There is no joy in that."

"Of course not, my dear Maggie. But you're only seventeen. Life holds many joys and mysteries yet ahead for you. I know things seem bleak to you today, but the war isn't over. Just this one battle is lost."

"Fiona is lost to me." Maggie's heart clenched with pain at even uttering the words.

"No, she's not, my dear. Even if she lives with Leora, you'll still see her. You're part of our family, too."

"But what if the judge rules Leora can keep Fiona forever?"

"Forever is a long time. You'll always be sisters and love one another. I'll prevail upon Leora to allow you to see her anytime you wish."

Maggie shook her head. "It's not the same. But sure, and your daughter will have Fiona calling her mum before I can turn around. Fiona will never hear the stories of our own mum and fa. She'll forget all about being an O'Keefe."

"All I can say is that I will do my best for you both, Maggie. But you must try to go on with life instead of wallowing in this room." Her voice was firm. "That's enough moping. We must be off before our daylight is gone. We've already wasted most of the morning. I don't want to impose on our friends and neighbors any longer than I have to. Simon stopped by while you were up here and said the carpenter would be at the house in an hour. I mean to have some of the mess cleaned up by then. Now come along."

Maggie forced herself to her feet. She wrapped her shawl tighter around her shoulders. She didn't want to face anyone, but the woman would give her no peace. The stress of the past few days had left her exhausted and lethargic. She didn't know where she would find the strength to work today. Her legs and arms felt heavy as the iron Fa used to weld.

Abigail smiled. "Good girl. You'll be a great help to me today." She chattered as Maggie followed her down the stairs. Sally was reading the children a story as they passed through the parlor. Maggie found an umbrella for Abigail, then dragged her shawl up over her own head. The rain wouldn't hurt her shorn hair.

They hurried up Miami Street hill toward the Masters home on Hill Street. Daylight showed the devastation from the night before. Limbs littered the walk and the streets; roofs showed areas bare of shingles; shutters hung crookedly from broken windows. Glass from those same windows crunched beneath their feet.

Maggie was unable to hold back the gasp of dismay when she saw the once-beautiful home. The entire pitched roof was missing. The upper outline was now a flat line of floor. Nearly every window was gone. The magnificent oak that had shielded the front porch from both the winter wind and summer sun lay across the street in front of the house. Part of the front porch was missing as well. The great house looked old and battered.

Abigail put a hand to her throat, and Maggie saw her struggling to hold back the tears.

"Well," she said finally, "we have our work before us." She marched up the walk, stepping gingerly over the debris, until she stood before the front door. She drew in a sharp breath, then pushed open the door.

Maggie followed her into the entry. It was even worse than she remembered. The beautiful parquet floors were water-stained, and glass and debris were everywhere.

"The dustbin is in the pantry," Abigail said. She shook the water off her skirts, then leaned the umbrella against the doorjamb to dry and rolled up her sleeves. "I'll tackle the parlor while you sweep the entry and the dining room. We'll soon have this right."

Maggie hurried to do as she was told, though she secretly thought it would take many more hands than they possessed to find what was left of the house. This rain would soak everything, leaving plaster walls damaged and rugs and furniture ruined.

But she diligently swept up the glass, sticks, and leaves into a pile, then hauled the piles to the dustbin.

Simon interrupted her as she was washing the dishes left when they had all rushed to the basement. "It seems a lost cause, doesn't it?"

Maggie jumped. "But sure, and you frightened me! This rain muffles everything so."

Simon frowned. "It had better stop soon, or we'll have even more trouble. The river is rising fast, and the town could flood. I've seen water nearly as far as Canal Street."

Maggie shuddered. "I cannot swim. I hope it does not come any farther, or me home will be flooded. And the carpenter hasn't come yet." She had thought things couldn't get any worse. Maybe she was wrong.

"I brought him. Mother is showing him around. He brought a wagonload of tarps to cover the top of the house and try to keep as much water out as he can. I have several men rounded up to help. They should be here any minute."

Simon's stare made Maggie feel self-conscious. "What is it? Do I have dirt on me nose?" she said finally. Her stomach was in knots, and she couldn't erase the way she'd felt last night in Simon's arms.

His eyes widened, and he grinned. "Sorry. Was I staring? You look lovely today, Maggie. I'm getting used to your short hair."

Heat flooded Maggie's face. "But sure, and I think you've kissed the Blarney stone!" She rubbed her short hair. " 'Tis hideous, I know. But it will grow." Warmth flooded her at his words.

"You could never be hideous, Maggie." Simon came closer and touched her hair with a light touch. "It's as soft as it looks. And so curly."

Maggie felt as though her tongue had stuck fast to the roof of her mouth.

"I talked to my lawyer friend today," he said.

Maggie caught her breath. "What did he say?"

"We could try to persuade the court to make Fiona a ward of someone who would allow her to stay with you and supervise her care. Or you could be married."

"M–married?"

Simon's eyes were somber, and he nodded.

Maggie felt as though she couldn't breathe. In that moment she knew she wanted nothing more from her life than to marry the man standing before her. She loved the way he studied a situation before making a decision, the way he had of standing with his hands in his pockets, the little cowlick on the left side of his head. Most of all she loved his steadfastness. Once he loved a woman, he would be committed to her and to her only, for the rest of his life. A woman would never have to wonder where she stood with Sheriff Simon Masters.

That woman would be the luckiest woman in the world. And it wouldn't be Maggie O'Keefe. Unshed tears burned Maggie's throat, and she quickly turned away.

Simon put a hand on her arm. "What is it, Maggie?

Did I say something wrong?"

She shook her head. " 'Tis nothing. A dust mote in me eye." She blinked desperately. If she cried now, she would never be able to hold her head up again.

Simon moved toward her, but a pounding at the front door stopped him.

"Sheriff! Come quick! The river is flooding!" a man's voice called from the front porch.

Maggie's heart lurched. Fiona! Then she realized her sister would be safe out on the Bickwells' farm. Simon took off at a run and threw open the door. Maggie followed him. From their vantage spot on Hill Street, Maggie could see the muddy floodwaters surging up Miami Street. The water was almost to Canal Street. People were streaming up the hill to escape the flood.

"Run over to the church and ring the bell," Simon told Maggie. "We need all the help we can get."

Maggie nodded and snatched up her shawl. Pulling it over her head, she ran out the door, dashed through the driving rain to the church down the street, and hurried inside. After several false tries, she found the door to the bell tower and climbed the wooden steps. Grasping the rope with both hands, she pulled with all her might. The bell began to ring in a frantic song of danger.

Maggie rang the bell until her hands were raw. Surely that was enough. She rubbed her throbbing hands together, then hurried downstairs and back to the Masters house. Abigail was gone, evidently joining in evacuating the residents of the low-lying areas.

For a moment Maggie was tempted to run, to fetch Fiona again and run as far and as fast as she could go.

Everyone would be busy for days cleaning up from the storm and the flood. But she couldn't do it, to Fiona or to herself. She was tired of running. They needed roots, she and Fiona. And if those roots meant they weren't together, then that was the cost they would both have to bear.

Dragging her shawl back over her hair, she stepped off the porch and ran down the hill toward town. She could help, too. The wind drove the rain in her face, and she could hardly see as she staggered over tree limbs and made her way downtown. She saw several rowboats on the surging waters as men struggled to reach stranded citizens. Was Simon out on those dangerous waters? Maggie hoped not; but knowing Simon as she did, she thought he would likely be in the midst of the action.

She hurried into her house and found Sally and the children peering out the windows at the floodwaters. She paused long enough to greet them, then dashed to the back room. She had Fa's old slicker and matching hat back here somewhere. Pawing through an old trunk on the back porch, she found what she was looking for and pulled them out with a cry of triumph. She dragged on the slicker and hat, then rushed out the door again, ignoring Sally's call to stop.

The waters had risen even more when she managed to make her way to Canal Street. She stopped in at the Boston General Store to find out where those being evacuated were to go, then went back out into the storm. As the rowboats deposited soaking wet men, women, and children to safety, she directed them to the church and to other homes where they might find shelter.

Through the long day she didn't catch sight of Simon,

but she felt somehow close to him as she worked in the driving rain. At least Fiona was out of this mess. Her sister was far from this river running over its banks. By five o'clock the rain finally stopped, though the water continued to rise. But most of the rowboats came in and stayed in. The people were safe, and that was all that mattered. The homes could be repaired and rebuilt.

She heard a familiar voice and turned as Simon stepped onto a railing and stood above the crowd. "Thank you all for your help. The danger is past for now. The churches are open. Let's all find a place of worship where we can thank God that no one drowned today." He gazed out over the crowd as if searching for something. When his gaze rested on Maggie, he smiled. Had he been looking for her? The thought warmed her.

Mutters of approval were heard all around; then the crowd surged up Miami Street toward the biggest churches. Maggie found herself carried along by the crowd. She tried to fight her way through to get to Simon, but there was no escaping the intentions of the people. Shrugging in resignation, she followed the crush of people to the church the Masters family attended on Hill Street. Most of the pews were filled by the time she stepped through the doors.

Leaning in the far back corner, Maggie closed her eyes. She would rest here until they were finished, then go home. She was grateful no one had drowned, but God didn't want to hear praises from the likes of her. He would be glad to hear them from the others, but she didn't think it was right to call on God for help when she ignored Him the rest of the time. This was only the third time she'd set foot inside a church. What did she know of praise?

The melodious peals of the organ filled the room, and Maggie drank in the lovely sound. In that moment she wished she knew how to pray, how to praise. Shrinking farther into the corner, she tried to be inconspicuous.

Then the congregation began to sing "A Mighty Fortress Is Our God," and the majestic strains filled Maggie's head with words she'd never heard before.

> A mighty fortress is our God,
> A bulwark never failing;
> Our helper He amid the flood
> Of mortal ills prevailing.

A bulwark. That's what she needed. Her great need for God crashed in on her in that moment. She'd been too proud to admit her need before. She wanted to do it all on her own, to care for Fiona and herself, to make her mark in the world and make Mum and Fa proud of her. She'd thought the reason she'd never come to God before was because she wasn't good enough. But it was pride that had kept her from God.

Tears flooded her eyes, and she struggled not to sob aloud. *I need You, God. I can't go on alone any longer. Save me, Jesus, or I die.* Mum had talked about Jesus. Maggie knew He had died on the cross for her, but all this time she had been convinced she needed no sacrifice. She could carry her own weight. But that wasn't true. She was helpless before God and His power.

The music went on and on, filling Maggie's soul with

light and hope and joy. When the last chords from the organ ended and the people stepped outside into the starlit sky, Maggie O'Keefe was a different person from the lonely stranger who had entered the church that night.

fourteen

Simon glanced at Maggie sitting beside him in the pew. Her face was turned up to the minister as she listened to the sermon. Something seemed different about her these past few days. When he stopped to escort his mother and the children to church, he'd been astonished and delighted to find Maggie prepared to attend as well.

The joy on her face all morning had made him wonder if she was beginning to see her need for God. How he prayed that was so and not his own blind desire. He'd thought about marriage ever since Robert had suggested it. But he was so uncertain about Maggie and her feelings. Even if she became a Christian, he wasn't sure about declaring how he felt. He didn't want a wife who agreed to marry him merely to keep her sister with her. He wanted Maggie's love, wholly and unfettered by convenience. How could he ever know for certain? He suppressed a sigh and dragged his attention back to the sermon. He'd have to leave it in God's hands. Only God's wisdom could sort it all out.

When the service was over, Simon escorted the ladies and the children back to his mother's. They had moved back in the day before, but they still had much work to do. The worst of the debris had been cleared away, however, and the windows repaired. The roof would take several weeks to reconstruct, though tarps kept the weather out for now, and the plaster walls upstairs needed work. But all in all they had been fortunate.

After the meal Simon sat beside Maggie on the sofa. "Would you like to drive out to visit Fiona this afternoon?"

Her face lit with joy. "But sure, and you would not need to ask that question!" She sprang to her feet. "Can we go now?"

He grinned. "The buggy is ready and waiting, milady." He offered his arm, and she gave him a smile that warmed him. He picked up her shawl from the hall tree and draped it over her shoulders. "I'll have her back by dusk, Mother," he called out.

It was a fine day. The birds sang in the sunshine, and puffs of clouds drifted lazily across the blue sky. The grass was greening, and the daffodils in his mother's front yard were shooting up to lift their faces to the sun. Driving out of town, he was filled with a sense of well-being and happiness. This was what he wanted, to have Maggie beside him always. But until he knew where she stood spiritually, she was off limits.

Maggie lifted her face to the sun as his mother's daffodils had done. She was even lovelier than the flowers, though. Her face, with its dusting of faint freckles across the bridge of her nose, was creamy with a hint of color on her cheeks. Her red hair gleamed in the sunlight, and her green eyes sparkled with life and zest. It was hard to keep from staring at her, to keep his mind on controlling the horse.

"You seem different lately, Maggie," he said. "Happier somehow. Or are you just excited about seeing Fiona?"

Maggie laughed. " 'Tis a rare day to be alive, I'm thinking. It's as though God is smiling down on us today."

Simon's heart thumped at the mention of God. "You seemed to enjoy the sermon," he said tentatively.

"But sure, and Pastor Timmons is a fine preacher. Me mum used to tell me Bible stories, but we never went to listen to preaching. Fa wouldn't allow it. He always said religion was a crutch, and only a weak man needed a crutch. He was no weak man, me fa. But lately I'm thinking he was weaker than he knew. Weak with pride and self-confidence. 'Tis a shame to learn such things about me fa." She fell silent, her face pensive. Then she smiled again. "I want to learn everything the Bible says."

"Why? You didn't seem interested a few weeks ago."

The color deepened in her cheeks, and she glanced at him, then down at the hands clasped in her lap. "But sure, and you'll think I'm crazy."

"No, I won't." Hope began a slow beat in his chest.

"Do you remember the day of the flood when everyone went to the church to praise God?"

He nodded. "I didn't see you there."

"Hiding in the corner I was. But I couldn't hide from God. When the music rang out, it was like God Himself spoke to me heart. I knew then that I needed Him in me life. And He answered." She turned a shining face up to him. "He answered the likes of Maggie O'Keefe." Awe was in her voice.

Simon tightened his hands on the reins to keep from clapping with sheer joy. "That's wonderful, Maggie. Did you tell Pastor Timmons? He would be glad to instruct you."

Maggie shook her head. "I'm saving me money to buy a Bible. I want to read it for meself. Not that I'm against learning what the preacher says," she added. "But I want to savor the words, to hear God speak them to me own heart."

"I have an extra Bible you can have. It was my grandma's, but I know she would have been glad for you to have it." It was all he could do to contain the words of love that wanted to spring from his heart. Now wasn't the time. She needed space and time to grow in the Lord. But maybe his dream would come true. Maybe Maggie could learn to love him for himself.

He turned into the track that led to his sister's farm. Stopping the buggy in front of his sister's house, he helped Maggie down, then escorted her to the front door. Inside they could hear squeals of laughter. Moments later Leora threw open the door. Her smile faded when she saw Simon and Maggie.

"Maggie!" Fiona ran through the doorway and threw herself against Maggie's skirt.

Maggie scooped her up. "But sure, and I think you're grown an inch since I've seen you, me girl. Have you been good?"

Fiona nodded. "Mama Leora made me a new dolly. Her name is Margaret. You want to see her?"

" 'Tis what I came for." Maggie put Fiona on the ground, and the little girl raced off.

"Aren't you going to invite us in?" Simon asked.

With obvious reluctance, Leora held the door open wider, and they stepped inside. "You didn't let me know you were coming. I'm not sure it's a good idea. Fiona is just settling down."

"But sure, and I can see that," Maggie said quietly.

"Your love and care I'll not be questioning."

Leora shrugged, but Simon could tell she was pleased by Maggie's praise.

"Can I get you some tea or coffee?" Leora asked.

Simon hid his surprise. "I'll have coffee, thanks."

"Nothing for me," Maggie said. She glanced around the parlor. " 'Tis a nice home you have."

"Thank you. Everett built it himself."

"Where is Everett?" Simon asked.

"A member of the Miami nation passed on this afternoon. He's with the family." Leora left the room and returned a few minutes later with Simon's coffee. "You and your coffee. I can't stand the stuff myself, but Everett is as bad as Simon."

Simon grinned and took the cup of coffee from her. Fiona came skipping back into the room with her dolly. She climbed on Maggie's lap and chattered excitedly about all she'd been doing. Slowly, the zest and joy seemed to leak out of Maggie like air out of a balloon. He knew she was wondering if she had the right to try to deprive Fiona of the happiness she seemed to have with a new mother and father. His own doubts resurrected. Fiona was as happy and content as he'd seen any child. Leora had the child calling her Mama already.

The afternoon shadows lengthened. Simon stood and stretched. "Well, I guess we'd better be heading for home."

Fiona stopped and looked up at Maggie. "Am I going home with you, Maggie?"

Pain etched Maggie's face, and she shook her head. "Not yet, me girl. You're going to stay here with your dollies and your nice toys. M—Mama Leora is taking good care of you." She stopped, and Simon saw her jaw clench. "I'll be back to see you soon."

"Okay." Fiona got down and skipped over to take hold of Leora's hand.

Only Simon saw the tears in Maggie's eyes as he helped her into the buggy. Leora and Fiona waved good-bye from the doorway; then Leora shut the door. Simon shook the reins, and the buggy jerked away. As soon as Fiona was no longer looking, Maggie clutched her arms around herself and began to rock back and forth.

Her eyes were dry, but Simon saw the desolation in their depths. " 'Tis clear I cannot drag her away from there," she whispered. "Cruel it would be. She calls Leora her mama. And sure, but why wouldn't she? Fiona has no memories of our own dear mum. But me wee one deserves a mum and a fa of her own. 'Tis clear I can't give her that."

Simon wanted to tell her he would be privileged to be Fiona's fa, but the words wouldn't come. "The final hearing is next week. Let's not give up hope yet, Maggie."

She shook her head. "I must pray and ask God for wisdom, Simon. Perhaps this is His will. I must not be selfish. Fiona's life and future are too important for that."

Simon nodded, and they left the farm far behind. He wished he could leave her pain behind as easily.

❧

Maggie didn't know what to do. As the days ticked by and the day of the hearing grew closer, she still didn't know. Should she fight or resign herself to the inevitable? And what did she have to offer Fiona that could compare with the stable home she now enjoyed with Everett and

Leora? She didn't want to be selfish. Fiona was too important for that.

The day before the hearing, Abigail sent her out to prune the rose bed. Maggie's heart was heavy. The children next door, Rebecca and Winnie, were clustered around their mother, Bridget, as she told them their morning Bible story. Maggie enjoyed these times as much as the children.

"Have either of you heard of Solomon?" Bridget asked.

Rebecca raised her hand. "He was the wisest man in the world," she said. "God offered to give him anything he wanted, but he didn't want wealth or anything else. He wanted wisdom."

"Very good, Rebecca," her mother said. "I'm going to tell you a story about Solomon. One day two women came to him. They carried a baby, and both women said the baby belonged to them."

Her chore forgotten, Maggie turned to listen.

"We'll call them Cassie and Dolores. Cassie claimed Dolores had stolen her baby in the night. Dolores's baby had died, Cassie said, and she had put the dead baby in place of Cassie's own child. But Cassie knew her own child, she said. And the dead child was not hers but belonged to Dolores. Dolores said no, the live baby was hers."

"What did King Solomon do?" Rebecca asked.

"He was very wise. He called for his guard to cut the baby in two and give each mother half."

The children gasped. "No, he wouldn't do that!" Rebecca said, putting her hands over her eyes.

Maggie leaned forward in dread. Would God allow a

man to do something like that? And how could Solomon be called wise if he did it?

The mother's voice grew more solemn. "The guard came forward and drew his sword. Then Cassie threw herself before King Solomon and begged him not to hurt the child. She said she would withdraw her claim to the baby and Dolores could have him. Dolores said yes, to cut the child in two. That's when King Solomon knew the truth. He knew Cassie was the real mother. How did he know?"

After a long silence, Winnie raised her hand. "Because Cassie was willing to give him up to save him?"

"Exactly," her mother said. "That's called sacrifice— when you love someone so much you're willing to hurt yourself if it's better for the one you love. That's how your daddy and I love you. And that's how Jesus loves us."

Maggie turned back to her rose bushes. Her heart was in turmoil. Was this what God expected of her? Could she even do it? Her mum and fa would be so angry with her. They had expected her to care for Fiona, not to give her away. She sank to the soft ground and clasped her arms around her. No, she couldn't do it. She wasn't strong enough. Surely God wouldn't ask it of her.

Shuddering, she forced herself to continue pruning the roses, but her mind wasn't on her chore. She pricked her finger on a thorn. Staring at the blood welling up on her finger, she realized again how much Jesus had given up for her. This sacrifice she would do for Fiona wouldn't involve blood, but it would take every bit of courage Maggie possessed, and the pain would be greater than anything she had borne so far.

Her way was suddenly clear. She had to do this, though it caused her heart to ache. The certainty grew, and Maggie shuddered. "If it be Your will, Lord, 'tis sure I must try to obey," she whispered finally. Once the decision was made, a peace fell on Maggie. It had to be done. Someday Fiona would thank her. As she worked in the garden all afternoon, she prayed for strength to do what was necessary.

After supper she went out to sit on the porch. A familiar form came up the walk.

"Mind if I join you?" Simon asked.

If he only knew how her heart soared when he was around. But she merely smoothed her skirt and nodded.

He sat in the rocker next to her. "Are you ready for tomorrow?"

It was so like him to be concerned. " 'Tis glad I am that you've come. I've reached a decision about tomorrow."

"What kind of decision?"

"I'm going to withdraw me request to keep Fiona with me."

Maggie could feel his shock in the silence. Shock and something else. Some kind of tension.

"I wish you wouldn't, Maggie. I came over to talk to you about something," he said. He turned to face her. "I've given it a lot of thought, and I want to marry you. Together we can offer Fiona a stable home. She can grow up with brothers and sisters and lots of love."

For a moment Maggie allowed herself to dream of what it would be like to raise children with Simon, to look across the breakfast table at him every morning. She drew a shuddering breath. He hadn't spoken one word of love. That wasn't the kind of marriage she wanted. She wanted what her parents had. The way Fa touched Mum's shoulder, the little things he did for her. Simon pitied her. It was no basis for marriage.

She squared her shoulders. " 'Tis kind of you to offer, but I'm afraid I must decline, Simon. I've made up me mind. This is what's best for Fiona. You saw her with Leora. But sure, and wasn't she happier than you'd ever seen her? So bright and cheery with dollies to play with, a nice room, pretty clothes. And a mum and fa who doted on her." She jumped to her feet before the impending tears could escape her eyes. She wanted to shout at him, to tell him she would marry him if he could love her for herself and not just Fiona. But the words were closed in her throat.

"Maggie," Simon began, "together you and I can give her those things as well." He reached out his hand.

Maggie couldn't bear it. She knew herself well enough to know she might weaken. Simon started to speak again, but Maggie couldn't stand to see the pity in his face. She threw open the door and rushed to her room.

ஐ

Simon strode back toward the apartment above his office. He'd handled that badly. Not one word of love had passed his lips. And after all his agonizing over whether Maggie could love him for himself and not as a way to save Fiona, he had talked only of making a home for Fiona! He groaned and slammed the door behind him.

His deputy looked up. "You look like someone just shot your horse. What's eating you?"

Simon dropped into the chair beside Sam. "I took one

look at those green eyes of Maggie's, and all I could do was stumble over the words. I want to marry her, but she thinks I just want to save Fiona for her. She turned me down flat."

Sam grinned. "Makes chasing a bank robber seem like a stroll along the river, don't it, Sheriff? I'd rather ride a bucking bronco than go through that again. I don't have no good advice for you. But women like sweet talk and flowers. Did you try flowers?"

Simon groaned again and put his hands over his face. "I didn't think of flowers. You think that might help?" Just the thought of everyone in town seeing him, the sheriff, carrying flowers made his face warm.

"Sure thing. Or a ribbon for her hair. 'Course little Maggie don't got much hair for ribbons right now. But she's a pretty thing, and she's got you lassoed."

Simon sighed. "Is it that obvious?"

Sam shrugged. "If you call getting calf-faced every time she walks in the room obvious, then it is. But then I know you pretty good. When's the wedding?"

Didn't Sam hear him? "I asked her to marry me, and she turned me down, Sam. Flat. Of course I just pointed out I could offer her and Fiona a home. I was too chicken to tell her I loved her."

Sam hit Simon over the head with his hat. "What were you thinking, Sheriff? Women like flowery words and poetry, stuff like that."

Poetry? This was getting worse by the minute. Next Sam would be telling him he had to *write* poetry! "Now what do I do?"

"You run over to the Boston Store and buy her a

pretty ribbon for her hair. Stop by my house and pick her some flowers. Tell my wife I sent you. Then trot yourself back over there and tell her you must have been crazy not to mention you think she hung the moon."

"I can't say stuff like that, Sam! What would she think?" Simon's face grew hot just to think of the pity in Maggie's face if he acted so crazy.

"She'll say yes, that's what she'll say, Sheriff. I've seen the way she looks at you. That girl's in love with you. You're just too lug-headed to see it."

"You're right. I'm going to march in there and tell her I love her." Simon stood. His pulse raced, but it was from excitement not fear. He could do this. He'd just handled it wrong before. "Thanks, Sam," he said before striding to the door and heading for the store.

But he'd failed to calculate the time. The store was closed, and so was every other one that might carry ribbons. Would just flowers work? He frowned. He wanted to do this right. The morning would be soon enough.

But the next morning when he was about to head out, a passerby dashed in to tell him a robbery was in progress at the bank. Buckling on his gun and grabbing a rifle, Simon raced to the bank. By the time he'd interrupted the robbery and arrested the two men, it was three hours later. Looking at his watch, he realized the hearing was about to start. And he had to charge the men and get them to jail. *God, be with her,* he prayed. He wished he could be. But he would get there as soon as he could.

fifteen

Maggie dressed carefully, then went down the steps.

"Do you want me to come with you, Maggie?" Abigail asked. "And are you sure you want to do this?"

" 'Tis sure I am. It's for the best. You and I both know it. And I need to do this alone."

The older woman bowed her head. "I'll be praying for you, my dear."

She had tried to talk her out of her decision the previous evening, but Maggie had held firm. She knew what she had to do, and she would do it. No matter what it cost her.

Maggie nodded. "I'll be back soon." She went out the door and down the street to the courthouse. Her legs felt weak as though they wouldn't hold her, and she felt flushed. But determined.

Leora and Everett were already in the courthouse when she arrived. Glancing around, Maggie's heart sank when she saw no sign of Simon. Fiona spied Maggie and jerked her hand out of Leora's, then ran to Maggie. Maggie knelt and put her arms around her sister. Holding the small body, she swallowed back a sob.

"Maggie, you're squeezing too tight," Fiona complained.

"Sorry, me darling." Maggie released her. "You look very pretty, Fiona."

The little girl smiled broadly. "Mama Leora made my

dress. Isn't it pretty? I like pink." She touched Maggie's face. "But I like the dress you made for Christmas better. It's pink, too."

Maggie swallowed the lump in her throat and smiled her thanks at Leora. She smoothed the red curls from Fiona's face. "You love your new mama, don't you, Fiona?"

Fiona nodded. "And Papa Everett. He gives me horsey rides on his knee." She flung her arms around Maggie's neck. "But I love you best, Maggie."

She'd never given her sister horsey rides. They'd never had time for that. Maggie drew a deep breath. "I think you should stay with your new mama and papa forever, Fiona."

She heard a slight gasp from Leora. Maggie glanced over at her, and their eyes met. Everett began to smile. Leora held her hand to her mouth, but her eyes were full of tears. Her gaze went to Everett, and the tenderness in their faces convinced Maggie she was doing the right thing.

"Forever?" A frown wrinkled Fiona's small face.

"Wouldn't you like that? I'll come out to see you sometimes, but you'll get to stay in your pretty room with your new mama and papa." Every word she spoke was an effort. It was all she could do not to break into tears, to gather Fiona close and run from the courtroom with her.

"I want to come home with you!" Tears began to pool in Fiona's eyes, but Maggie steeled her heart. Fiona didn't understand that this was for the best.

"I promise I'll see you all the time." The child didn't have to know now that it wouldn't be often. For Maggie had realized in the night that she couldn't bear to stay in Wabash. With Fiona and Simon both lost to her, she needed to start fresh somewhere else. All she needed was a small room somewhere and enough money for food. Without Fiona to care for, success was no longer important.

Fiona continued to cry, but Maggie thrust her into Leora's arms, then stood and squared her shoulders as the judge was seated.

"Are we ready to hear the case?" he asked.

"Your honor, there will be no case," Maggie said. "Fiona has a new family. I'm withdrawing me petition to care for her." With that she turned and ran from the room. Her heart throbbed with pain, and she dared not look back at Fiona.

Escaping the courthouse, she leaned against a post and squeezed her eyes shut. Her breath rasped in her throat as she fought for control. Taking a deep breath, she opened her eyes and walked purposefully toward the Masters house and orphanage. She would sneak up the back stairs and leave the note she'd written for Abigail on her bed. The sooner she was gone from here, the sooner the pain would go away.

The house was quiet as she slipped in the back door and tiptoed up the stairs. The third step from the top creaked, and she stopped, her hand to her mouth. But no one said anything, and she crept down the hall. After leaving the note, Maggie took her valise of hand-me-down clothing Abigail had given her and slipped back outside.

Abigail had been kind enough to pay her a small pittance, in addition to her room and board, and Maggie had saved every penny. If she was careful, she could buy a train ticket back to Logansport and ask for her old job back. With God's help, maybe her old room would even be available. Then, when the pain wasn't so fresh, she could come back to visit Fiona once in awhile. Logansport wasn't that far away.

She didn't think anyone would come looking for her. They all knew she was competent to earn a living and take care of herself. It felt strange not to worry about Fiona any longer. But she knew Leora and Everett would take good care of her.

Maggie squeezed aboard the train, and it pulled out without incident. A wave of nostalgia and longing swept over her as the town faded from her view. She'd thought it might be home. And it would always hold the two people Maggie held most dear: Simon and Fiona.

What would Simon do when he discovered her missing? Probably nothing. She had thrown his marriage proposal back in his face. Why would he chase after her? It would be one less problem for him to worry about.

When she disembarked in Logansport a few hours later, she had the beginning of a sniffle. Or maybe it was just the effects of holding back the tears all day. Wearily, she made her way to Watson's Mercantile.

Norma Watson was behind the counter. Her broad face creased in a smile when she saw Maggie. "Well, if it isn't our Duffy Ogan. Or should I say Maggie O'Keefe." She came around the counter and hugged Maggie. "What are you doing back in town?"

"Looking for a job again, Mrs. Watson. Would you be hiring?"

"Funny you should ask that. I was making up a sign for a shop girl. And it includes room and board. I have a room over the mercantile I cleared out. It isn't much, but it has a bed and a few pieces of furniture. The job's yours if you want it."

Thanks to the good Lord, Maggie thought with relief. " 'Tis grateful, I am, Mrs. Watson."

"You going to run off with that sheriff again?" Mrs. Watson asked with a twinkle in her eye. "Not that I'd blame you. He's a handsome cuss."

Maggie swallowed the lump that formed in her throat at the mention of Simon. "No, he's back in Wabash, and that's where he's likely staying. If he would happen to come looking for me, please don't tell him I'm here."

"It's like that, is it?" Mrs. Watson's shrewd gaze sharpened, and she nodded.

" 'Tis like that," Maggie said quietly.

"Well, don't just stand there with your mouth letting in the flies. Put your things upstairs and get to work."

Rejoicing in God's provision, Maggie scurried up the stairs and deposited her valise on the narrow bed. Taking time for a quick glimpse around the room, she noticed it was bare save for the bed, a stand with a pitcher and bowl, and a single chair by the window. But it would do. She went downstairs to get to work.

The store was busy, and one day flowed into another. Before Maggie realized it, she had been there nearly a week. She was thankful for the work. Too tired at night to do more than read the Bible Simon had given her, she would fall into bed and sleep too soundly to dream of what might have been with Simon.

She prayed often for Fiona and for Simon. As long as they were happy, she could be content. But her heart was bruised and lonely, in spite of Norma Watson's friendliness. Wabash would always be her home in her heart. She hoped someday to put this all behind her and have a family of her own, but it was a faint hope. Only Simon made her heart sing.

Sunday morning she washed her face and ran a comb through her short curls. She was thankful they were beginning to grow out. Maybe soon the stares at her hair would cease. Now she had to find a church. Mrs. Watson had informed her she was a God-fearing woman but not a church-goer. Maggie didn't want to push her yet, but she intended to try to find a good church, then talk the older woman into attending with her.

Pushing open the front door, she was almost knocked over by a man. The sun was in her eyes, and she couldn't see his face, but something about the breadth of his shoulders set her heart pounding.

"Maggie."

There was no mistaking that voice. She placed her hands on her hips. "But sure, and I suppose you're showing up now to drag me off to court again? What are the charges this time, Sheriff?"

His firm fingers gripped her elbow, and he drew her inside the mercantile. "Theft."

Theft? Maggie's mouth dropped open. She had never stolen anything in her life. Out of the glare of the sun, she was able to study his face. A look of strain shadowed his eyes. In one hand he held flowers. Incredulous, Maggie stared at the flowers, then back up at Simon.

"Now you listen here, Maggie O'Keefe, and you listen good. These flowers are for you." He thrust them into her hand.

She stared at the lilacs. Their sweetness filled the air, and she buried her nose in them. "Th—thank you, Simon. But what's this about theft?"

"Did you think I would shirk my duty? I couldn't let you get by with petty thievery. Though in this case, it's a pretty serious offense and not petty at all."

Her anger sparked, and she drew back from him. "I wouldn't take a nickel that didn't belong to me, and you know it, Simon Masters. Whoever it is that has accused me is lying! And you know that as well."

She slanted a look at Simon and caught an expression of consternation on his face. His tanned face flushed, he nevertheless met her gaze with a direct stare of his own. Maggie felt her own face flush with heat. She was confused.

"It's not a lie," he said. "You're a thief, all right. And I'll tell you about it in my own good time."

Maggie didn't know what to say. Something was going on here that she didn't understand. Simon was so ill at ease, yet intent. "How—how is Fiona?" she asked.

"Fine. She said to give you a kiss."

Before she could even react to his words, his arms came around her, and his head came down to meet hers. The touch of his lips against hers left her weak. The flowers slipped from her fingers and fell to the floor.

She had told herself that if he ever kissed her again, she would behave in a more cautious fashion, but her arms seemed to creep around his neck of their own volition.

His arms tightened around her, and she never wanted the kiss to end. In his arms she felt safe and protected. Nothing could touch her with Simon beside her.

Maggie sighed when he pulled away. She laid her head against his chest and listened to the beat of his heart under her ear. "What did I steal?" she whispered.

He tilted her head up so their gazes met. "My heart. You took it when I wasn't looking. I had to come find you. I botched it all the other night, Maggie. I love you. That's why I want to marry you. Not for Fiona's sake, but for my sake. All I ask is that you give yourself a chance to love me. I'm not a romantic man." He picked up the flowers and handed them to her again. "These flowers were Sam's idea; he said women love flowers and poetry. I don't know any poetry, but I do know I love you."

Twice. He said he loved her twice. It must be true. Maggie stared into his face and saw the tenderness there. She must be dreaming. She reached up her hand and caressed his cheek.

"But sure, and what would I do with fancy words like poetry? The flowers are nice, though." She buried her nose in the lilacs. "Lilacs are my favorite."

"Do you think you could care for me, Maggie? I know you're young, and I'm nearly ten years your senior, but I promise no man would cherish you more than I do."

Cherish. What a lovely word. No one had ever used it around her before, and certainly not *about* her. She wanted to hug the word to herself.

Simon turned his head so his lips met the palm of her

hand that had been lying against his cheek. Pressing his lips against it, he spoke into her hand. "Do I have a chance, Maggie?"

"Aye, you have more than a chance, me boyo," she whispered. "But sure, and don't I love you already? I love your sense of justice and right and wrong. I love the way you are so thoughtful with your mum and with the ladies at the church."

"Does that mean you'll marry me?" he put in eagerly.

She laughed, a joyous sound that delighted even herself. "It's no choice I'll be having now, is it? Me heart won't let me make the mistake of turning you down again."

"I'm glad you agreed before I had to use unusual pressure."

"What unusual pressure?"

His grin widened. "I have a surprise for you." He stepped to the door and pushed it open. Fiona raced inside and flung herself against Maggie's skirts. Leora followed slowly, her face more animated than Maggie had ever seen before. Her smile even seemed genuine.

Maggie swept Fiona into her arms. Her heart thumped against her ribs as her gaze traveled from Simon to his sister. What was going on?

Leora touched Maggie's hand. "I had to come, Maggie. God has gotten hold of my heart and shown me how selfish and cruel I've been. I have no right to take Fiona from you. You've done a fine job of raising her. I must have been a little mad for a time. But God showed me I was wrong. Can you ever forgive me?"

Emotion closed Maggie's throat, and she couldn't say

a word. Leora's gaze searched her own until Maggie finally managed to speak. "I—I forgive you," she whispered. "But sure, and who could resist Fiona?"

Leora's face softened. "That's so true." She reached out and touched the little girl's hair. "I'll miss her dreadfully. I hope you'll bring her to visit her——her auntie." Tears filled her eyes, and she stepped back.

"But sure, and you'll get tired of seeing us," Maggie said softly.

Leora managed a tremulous smile. "I'm going to take Simon's advice and adopt a needy child from Mama's orphanage. I've been too pigheaded about that as well." She drew a shaky breath. "Well, I'd best be going. Everett is waiting outside in the buggy. We'll see you back in Wabash." Tears welled in her eyes, and she hurried away.

Simon sighed. "Guess you have to marry me now. Fiona needs a daddy." He brushed his fingers across Maggie's cheek and slipped his arms around both her and Fiona.

Mrs. Watson bustled down the steps. Stopping short when she saw Maggie in Simon's arms, she put her hands on her hips.

Shaking a finger at them, she took a step nearer. "You promised me the handsome sheriff wouldn't be spiriting you away again, Maggie. From the looks of things, I fear I'm about to lose my shop girl."

Simon released Maggie and stepped away a more circumspect distance, though he kept one arm around her. Maggie felt empty from that small distance. Her head was spinning from the enormity of what had happened, and she couldn't seem to stop smiling. Simon *and* Fiona. It was too good to be true.

"Sorry, Mrs. Watson," Simon said. "I admit it. I'm taking Maggie away. This time for good. She's agreed to be my wife."

"Humph. It's about time," Mrs. Watson muttered. "I knew right off you were too much of a man to let her get away." Her eyes shone with appreciation as she looked at Simon. She pursed her mouth. "Don't let me see you at my door again, Maggie O'Keefe. You take good care of your man, and don't go gallivanting off on your own again."

"I won't, Mrs. Watson," Maggie said. The way she felt right now, she never wanted to let Simon out of her sight.

"Get your things together," Simon said. "We can still make the next train if we hurry. Does Maggie owe you any money, Mrs. Watson?"

She squinted at him. "Nope. She worked her way, fair and square. I've never had a better worker than Maggie O'Keefe—unless it was that Duffy Ogan." She smiled. "That lad was a fine boy, I must say."

Maggie blushed at the reminder of her masquerade. She wished her hair would be grown out for the wedding, but she didn't want to wait that long, and she had a feeling Simon wouldn't be willing to wait, either. Chuckling, she handed Fiona to Simon, then rushed up the stairs and threw her few belongings into the valise. She'd hardly had time to settle in, and she was going back.

She wanted to dance and sing and whirl around the room with joy. But she merely picked up her bag and headed down the steps to join her beau. What a wonderful thought. She'd never had a beau before. She smiled as she listened to his deep voice teasing Mrs. Watson.

"You bring your family back for a visit now and again," Mrs. Watson admonished as she shooed them out the door. "And don't forget to send me an invitation to the wedding. I might surprise you and find someone to run the shop that day."

"We will." Maggie waved to her and started down the street with her hand tucked tenderly inside the crook of Simon's arm. He was holding Fiona securely in his other arm. She was going to marry Simon. The shock of it still hadn't left her. She wondered what his mother would say. Had Simon told her yet? She wanted to ask him, but if his mother wasn't happy about it, Maggie didn't want to know right now. She didn't want anything to mar the beauty of this moment. She would have her own home, she and Simon. They would raise a family, siblings for Fiona, and grow old together.

Simon squeezed her hand. "I'm so happy I could pop," he whispered. "I want to shout to the whole town that darling Maggie has agreed to be my wife. See how everyone stares? They're all envious of me. Mother is delighted."

That answered that question. "Hush," she murmured. Glancing around, she saw several smiles directed their way, and her cheeks grew hot. " 'Tis more likely they're saying to themselves how they can't believe that poor man is having to escort that woman with the shorn hair. I should make you wait until me hair grows before we have the wedding."

He leaned over and twirled a curl around his finger. "Did I ever tell you how lovely you are when you laugh, my Maggie? And I'm not waiting a minute longer than it takes to arrange a suitable wedding."

Maggie smiled at Simon and leaned her head against his shoulder. "But sure, and isn't May a lovely time for a wedding?"

epilogue

"I hate this hat!" Fiona yanked at the offending concoction of flowers and ribbon.

"Don't do that, Darling!" Leora adjusted the hat again and smiled an apology at Maggie. "Doesn't Maggie look beautiful, Fiona?"

Fiona stared at her sister through narrowed eyes, then nodded. "But why do I have to wear this hat?"

"Because it's a wedding hat," Leora said. She adjusted the hat, then turned to Maggie. "There. You look beautiful. It's time to go."

Maggie was ready to leave the room when the door opened and Margaret hurried in. "Wait!" she cried. In her arms she carried something white.

Maggie looked closer. Her mum's wedding gown! "Where did you find it?" she breathed.

"Someone found your trunk in a field," Margaret said. "Here—let's put it on you."

Maggie stepped quickly out of her plain blue gown and into her mother's. Then Margaret set the veil on Maggie's head. "Now you're ready to marry the town's most eligible bachelor," she said approvingly.

As the strains of the wedding march drifted down the hall for the third time, Margaret adjusted Maggie's veil. "You'd better go," she said smiling.

Fiona trooped in front of her with her basket of rose

petals. Following her sister, Maggie fixed her eyes on the man waiting for her at the other end of the aisle.

Simon moved forward to take her hand as she neared the front of the church. Tucking her fingers securely around his forearm, he stood with her before God and those assembled.

"Sure you're not making a mistake, Maggie?" he whispered as the minister stepped into place before them.

She gave him a tender look. "I've made plenty of mistakes in me life, Simon. And I'm sure many more are waiting for me. But this is not one of them." Secure in her love for Simon, all she could do was thank God for the mistake that had brought him into her life.

A Letter To Our Readers

Dear Reader:

In order that we might better contribute to your reading enjoyment, we would appreciate your taking a few minutes to respond to the following questions. We welcome your comments and read each form and letter we receive. When completed, please return to the following:

Rebecca Germany, Fiction Editor
Heartsong Presents
PO Box 719
Uhrichsville, Ohio 44683

1. Did you enjoy reading *Sonoran Sweetheart* by Nancy J. Farrier?

   ❑ Very much! I would like to see more books by this author!
   ❑ Moderately. I would have enjoyed it more if

   _____

   _____

2. Are you a member of **Heartsong Presents**? Yes ❑ No ❑
   If no, where did you purchase this book?_____

   _____

3. How would you rate, on a scale from 1 (poor) to 5 (superior), the cover design?_____

4. On a scale from 1 (poor) to 10 (superior), please rate the following elements.

   _____ Heroine   _____ Plot

   _____ Hero   _____ Inspirational theme

   _____ Setting   _____ Secondary characters

5. These characters were special because_____
_____

_____

6. How has this book inspired your life?_____
_____

_____

7. What settings would you like to see covered in future **Heartsong Presents** books?_____
_____

_____

8. What are some inspirational themes you would like to see treated in future books?_____
_____

_____

9. Would you be interested in reading other **Heartsong Presents** titles?　　　Yes ❑　　　　No ❑

10. Please check your age range:
　　❑ Under 18　　　❑ 18-24　　　　❑ 25-34
　　❑ 35-45　　　　❑ 46-55　　　　❑ Over 55

Name _____

Occupation _____

Address _____

City _____ State _____ Zip _____

Email _____

SWEET LIBERTY

Liberty—sweet liberty—can take many forms. How will God help four women find true freedom?

Four Historical Fourth of July Celebrations: *Freedom's Cry* by Pamela Griffin, *Free Indeed* by Kristy Dykes, *American Pie* by Debby Mayne, and *Lilly's Pirate* by Paige Winship Dooly.

paperback, 352 pages, 5 ³⁄₁₆" x 8"